VIRTUAL YOU!

# VIRTUAL YOU!

*Love, Beauty, Relationships, Purity, Truth*

## JIMMIE L. DAVIS

SERVANT PUBLICATIONS
ANN ARBOR, MICHIGAN

Vine Books is an imprint of Servant Publications especially designed to serve
evangelical Christians.

---

**Servant Publications—Mission Statement**
We are dedicated to publishing books that spread the gospel of Jesus Christ,
help Christians to live in accordance with that gospel, promote renewal in
the church, and bear witness to Christian unity.

---

Scripture quotations in this publication are from the New King James Version,
copyright 1979, 1980, 1982, Thomas Nelson, Inc., Publishers.

The names and characterizations in this book are fictional, although based on real
events. Any similarity between the stories and real people is unintended and purely
coincidental.

Published by Servant Publications
P.O. Box 8617
Ann Arbor, Michigan 48107
www.servantpub.com

Cover design: Brian Fowler, Grand Rapids, Mich.

02 03 04 05 10 9 8 7 6 5 4 3 2 1

Printed in the United States of America
ISBN 1-56955-305-X

## Dedication

To my sweet family
Sam, Jordan, Ginger, and Derek
for
Your support and prayers


Special thanks to all those who contributed to
the completion of this book:
Linda Gilden, Andrew Cavender, Dr. Allen Jackson, Iris Dobbins,
Candy Arrington, Michelle Van Ryssleburg,
Anna Duncan, Delaine Murray, Christie Huskey,
Lesa Banks, and Sarah Caldwell

# Contents

# Foreword

If you were a contestant on a game show like *Survivor* or *Moolah Beach*, you would take risks in hopes of winning an earthly reward. The contestants on these game shows must leave all that is familiar to them and do the challenging things the game host asks of them in order to win the big prize. Only one contestant or team can win the prize.

*Virtual You!* is not a game show, but like one, it asks you to take a risk, to step out in faith, and trust God with your entire life. You may have to leave behind all that gives you security and all that is familiar. Your Heavenly Father may ask you to do things that are challenging, but unlike the game show, *every* young woman who chooses to say yes to God and fall passionately in love with Jesus is *promised* more than just an earthly prize. Check out Jeremiah 29:11-12 and Proverbs 3:5-6.

I have spoken to thousands of women all over the world. Wherever I go, women have the same longings deep in their hearts, regardless of their age.

*Virtual You!* addresses these longings in a way that's unique to you as a young woman in your teen years. It helps you learn how to make wise decisions now that will keep you healthy spiritually, physically, emotionally, mentally, and relationally for a lifetime.

*Virtual You!* is a fun, interactive book that will cause you to think and discover the truth about who God is and what he wants to do in your life. Accept the life-changing challenges written in this book and enjoy your Prize (read Ephesians 1:16-19)!

Debby Jones
author of *Lady in Waiting*

# Introduction

I am happy you've chosen to join me in this incredible makeover experience. *Virtual You!* will help you change from the inside out. You will put on God's virtual glasses and take a look at yourself through his eyes. The best part about this whole experience is that God's makeover is a real miracle, not just an illusion.

We will study together, laugh and cry together, pray and grow together. You may like to take one chapter each week and use it as your daily Bible study time. Each chapter has a theme verse from God's Word for you to memorize. These verses will be marked by a small ♥ symbol. Copying the verses on index cards or sticky notes will be helpful. Keep the cards in a place where you will see them often.

Look up the verses and fill in the blanks for each chapter's study. You will only get as much out of this study as you put into it. Give God a chance! He loves you and wants to perform a miracle in your life.

Find a Christian adult mentor or college student you trust and ask her to lead you and several of your friends through this book. Finding a mentor is an important part of learning how to grow up. A mentor is someone who will come alongside and teach you from her life's experiences. A mentoring group is an awesome way to grow spiritually and to have fun in the process. There is a Leader's Guide in the back to assist her. It's great to share and discuss these topics with other girls who have the same problems, interests, and needs.

I suggest meeting together once a week to share and discuss what you have read at home. The discussion questions are marked with a ☺ symbol. You can meet in someone's home, at a local restaurant, or even at your church. You will not only grow closer to God, you will grow closer to those in your mentoring group. It's a great way to find God's plan for your life and to experience positive peer pressure at the same time.

Blessings as you grow together!
Jimmie Davis

## INSTANT MESSAGE

Guychasernumber1: Hi, I have a major question 4 U.

**VirtualYou77: Sure! What's up?**

Guychasernumber1: I like this guy in my English class. He is so cool! I've tried EVERYTHING to get him to like me, but he doesn't even know I'm alive. What can I do?

**VirtualYou77: Tell me what you have tried and we will go from there.**

Guychasernumber1: I've gotten a new hairdo. I bought new clothes that are really hot. I got my nails done. I go everywhere he goes. I'm outgoing so he will notice me. I even got one of my friends to tell him I like him! Nothing seems to work. HELP!

**VirtualYou77: Whoa, girl! You gotta get a grip. I think you're going about this thing all wrong. Let's see if we can help you think straight. That will change your actions and relationships.**

Guychasernumber1: Sounds good to me. What do I have to do?

# ONE

# Which Sticky Note Did I Write My Password On?

Have you ever forgotten your password? When I first got my computer I wrote my password down so I wouldn't forget it. Then I lost the sticky note! I couldn't log on; I couldn't check my E-mail; I couldn't chat with my friends! Passwords are important. A password is like a key. A key provides security and protection. A key can also provide freedom because it guards access to things that some people shouldn't be able to open—like your heart!

My sixteen-year-old son got his first set of keys to the family car a few months ago. He couldn't wait to go cruising with his friends. No more taggin' along with Mom! No more grocery store trips! No more bumming rides from friends! Freedom at last! Freedom to go wherever he wanted. Freedom to be independent. In what areas of your life would you like to have more freedom? ☺

_____

_____

_____

If you had more freedom, how do you think that would affect your attitudes and actions? ☺

_____

_____

As a teenager, I loved to write in my diary. I wrote "personal, private, die-if-anybody-found-out" things. I locked my diary and hid it in a box in the bottom of my closet behind the shoes I never wore. I kept the key on a chain around my neck. I took a shower with it and slept with it. That key gave me freedom. I had the freedom to write whatever I wanted, whenever I wanted, about whomever I wanted. I not only had freedom; I had protection. I could be "uncool" and nobody knew or thought I was weird. That key gave me security.

Today, you have all kinds of keys and passwords. The key to your locker, the password for your ATM card, the password for your voicemail, the key to your house, and the key to your car. All of these protect you and give you freedom.

What would happen if someone whom you could not trust got your password or took your key? Your security would be threatened. Your freedom would be gone. Your protection would be out the window.

What about your heart? Would you like to protect your heart during your teenage years? Wouldn't it be great to feel secure and not worry about what other people think? Would you like to have the freedom to be yourself? Most teens would, but they really don't know how to break free from the chains of peer pressure to freedom and security. Sometimes we feel a false sense of protection in going along with the crowd or being involved in a relationship with a guy. Sometimes a girl gives the key to her heart to a guy because she feels a sense of protection and security.

We all know there isn't a real key to your heart. It's a symbol of what it means to be careful about who controls your affection.

When that symbolic key is given to Jesus during your teen years, you will have freedom to be yourself. You will have the confidence to stand up for what is right. You will be secure, which gives you the freedom to enjoy your teenage years exactly the way God planned. Although the key is symbolic, the freedom and security are real.

When you give the key to your heart to Jesus, he protects your heart, gives you true freedom, and provides the ultimate security you need. Actually, he's the only One who can!

❤ Read Proverbs 4:23 and write the verse below. Also, write it on an index card and put it in an obvious place where you will see it often. Say it over and over until you have memorized the words.

_____

_____

_____

_____

_____

The Bible tells you to guard your heart because it affects everything you do. Your heart is fragile and easily broken. If you haven't discovered that yet, you probably will soon. When you give your heart to a guy who doesn't understand your deep heart needs, you may end up with a broken heart. It's hard to focus on enjoying life when your heart is broken. Guarding your heart is important because it determines how you function as a teenager.

Maybe you realize you should guard your heart, but you don't really know how. What do you do about the emptiness and longing in your heart for true love? Let's see if we can figure it out together.

## The Longing in Your Heart

Lauren grew up in a family where she never felt loved by either of her parents. She knew they must love her, but it seemed hard for them to show her. Her father's work seemed more important to him than she did. Often, she waited for him to show up, only to find that "something came up at work," leaving her disappointed again. Lauren's mom was a good mom, but she was consumed with her own problems.

At home, Lauren felt lonely. Her parents constantly argued. Usually, she ended up in her room with her CD player blasting to drown out their yelling.

Lauren was drop-dead gorgeous. Her long dark hair fell into a natural cradle around her slender face. Her dark almond-shaped eyes drew attention to her long lashes. She learned at an early age how to get the attention she needed. The flutter of her lashes and the sparkle in her eyes seemed to make most guys turn on their heels. The attention she received made the emptiness go away for a short time. But soon the sparkle would fade and the flutter would stop as the reality of her loneliness set in.

Lauren planned her whole day around her current crush. Each morning, she got up and tried on several outfits before finding the right look for her slender body. She meticulously applied her make-up, and her silky hair won the award for "most combed hair of the day." It wasn't hard to slip out the door wearing her micro-mini skirt because her mom was still asleep and her dad had already been at the office for hours.

She hurried to school, ran by the restroom to check her make-up, and then darted to the spot where her crush would pass at exactly

7:54 A.M. She spotted him coming down the hall, and her voice echoed through the crowd to catch his attention. As he approached, she took a step into his path where he was destined to run into her. Nonchalantly she said, "Oh, excuse me," and turned her head quickly, slinging her silky hair and giggling to her friends.

He said, "Oh, hi, Lauren," and headed on down the hall.

Her heart beat wildly as she squealed to her girlfriends, "Did you hear that? He said, 'Hi, Lauren.' I knowwww he likes me!"

She forgot about her emptiness for a time and floated to her first-period class. As the clock ticked away toward second period, she gathered her books, got on the mark, and when the bell rang, she was off! She ran the hundred-yard dash each morning to make it to his second-period class in time. He was usually in front of biology class one minute before the bell rang. She sped through the hallway, bumping kids right and left, never stopping to say excuse me. She planned in her mind what to say as she passed by him. It was a race against the clock to get two buildings away and back before the bell rang. Most of the time she made it just in time, but she had become very creative in making excuses since her first and second period classes were right beside each other.

Her day continued like this until evening. At home, she retreated to her room to busy herself in writing a note to give to a friend, to give to a friend, to give to him. She fell into bed each night exhausted from the day's adventure, only to get up the next morning with the same emptiness and start the process all over again. Can you identify with any part of Lauren's story? Name some similarities between Lauren's life and yours. ☺

_____

_____

_____

_____

_____

_____

Most girls admit to scheming for a guy's attention from time to time. Do you long to have someone love you? Do you find yourself criticizing your mom and dad because they have never been there for you? Most girls can identify with at least one small part of Lauren's story.

Like Lauren, do you spend all your waking hours trying to catch a guy? If so, have you ever asked yourself *why?* Take a wild guess and write it in the space.

_____

_____

_____

There are many reasons a girl feels it necessary to chase guys. It's almost like a sport. Many times a girl believes she has to take things into her own hands. Do you ever feel as if God will not give you someone? Or maybe you are not willing to wait on God's timing. Maybe you feel emptiness in your heart and think, "If I could just have a date with him, I would be so happy." Would that date make you happy long-term? Probably not. Sometimes a girl will give her heart to a guy who is not ready or mature enough to protect it. I heard a country western song once that insinuated some guys will "stomp on your heart and mash that sucker flat." Have you ever felt that way? If so, how did you handle the situation? ☺

_____

_____

_____

_____

_____

For whatever reason a girl feels as if she has to chase her guy, it all boils down to one word—insecurity. Insecurity can be defined as "the emptiness and longing you feel in your heart." (That's from my one-word dictionary.) Let's face it—every girl has felt insecure at times.

Maybe you think a guy can give you the security you need. It may be your daddy, a boyfriend, a teacher, a coach, or some guy you don't even know well. But the truth is that no one, not your daddy, not the guy you date, not the man you will marry someday, or anyone else, can give you true, lasting security—only Jesus can.

Whenever you try to fill your emptiness with anyone other than Jesus, you put unrealistic expectations on that person. You are asking him to do something impossible. You can think of it this way. Guys (dads, boyfriends, or husbands) range on a scale from 1 to 10. One represents lousy and ten represents awesome. Think of a significant guy in your life. It may be your dad, a boyfriend, or someone else who is important to you. Circle the number where he fits on the line below.

**1____2____3____4___5__6___7___8___9___10**
**Lousy**                   **Average**             **Awesome**

VIRTUAL YOU!

Most guys rate somewhere around average or above. But it doesn't matter where your guy rates on the scale, he still cannot meet the deepest needs of your heart. Actually, guys have the same emptiness and insecurity you have. That emptiness and insecurity began way back in the Garden of Eden with the first sin, and it has been passed down through the centuries like a mutated gene. (Your science teacher will be proud you can use that term in a sentence!) It's not a *guy* you are longing for in your heart. It's a relationship with God! The big problem is sin.

Sin separates you from a holy God. God is pure and holy and cannot be connected to evil. One of God's eternal laws is that sin must be punished. Read Romans 6:23 and write what the verse says in your own words.

_____

_____

_____

_____

God loves you so much he was willing to send his only Son, Jesus Christ, and accept his death as the wages, or payment, for your sin. Jesus died on the cross for the sins of every person. God sent Jesus to bridge the gap between you and God. Read Romans 10:9-10. What do these verses say you must do to be saved from your sins?

_____

_____

_____

_____

22

When you confess your sins (agree with God that you have done wrong) and believe in your heart that God sent Jesus to die for you, then you will be saved. Now Jesus is standing in the gap for you. Only you can make that decision to cross the bridge to your loving Heavenly Father.

Once you have accepted Jesus as your Savior, you can give him the key to your heart to keep in a safe place. When you are complete in Christ Jesus and totally secure in your relationship with him, then, and only then, can you have a balanced relationship with a guy. You can have the kind of relationship God planned when he made Eve to be a companion and helper to Adam. (We will talk more about how to accept Jesus into your life in the next chapter.)

Being secure in Christ gives me peace and comfort even in an insecure world. I have a wonderful husband, and I feel confident he will not walk out on me because he has a commitment to God and to the vows he made on our wedding day. But what if he died of a heart attack or was killed in an accident? If my security came from the fact that I had a husband, I would fall apart. Because I have security in my relationship with Jesus Christ, I would go on and fulfill God's plan for my life. I would miss my husband because I love him, but my life would continue with peace and comfort.

What if your father or a boyfriend has failed you or hurt you terribly? How can you respond to your hurt and anger? Think about the person who has hurt you. It may not be easy to do. Think about how you feel. Think about how disgusted and disappointed you feel at his actions.

Now think about your actions. Have you hurt God or failed God? How does God respond to you when you have failed him?

_____
_____
_____
_____
_____

Do you think God looks at you the same way you look at the person who has hurt you? No! God gives you grace when you have failed him. The definition of grace is giving you the good things you don't deserve. Once you have experienced God's grace and understand his forgiveness, you can begin to extend that same grace to those who have hurt you and failed you. Besides, forgiveness helps you; it does not necessarily help the person who has hurt you.

Pray now and ask God to show you any unforgiveness in your heart. Maybe you need to forgive your dad or someone else who has hurt you. Confess it to God and allow him to heal your hurts and help you forgive. Write your prayer to God in the space below. It is okay to use codes if it is something personal.

_____
_____
_____
_____

Maybe you have never allowed the Lord Jesus Christ to come into your heart and fill that emptiness you have. You can make a decision to ask Christ to come into your life and bridge the gap. You can ask him to forgive you of your sins and allow him to become your security. You can accept his forgiveness and extend that same forgiveness to the people who have hurt you. Many times a girl will ask Jesus to come into her heart, but not give him complete control over her life. Asking Jesus to come into your heart means you can give him the key to your heart, and that gives him complete control over your life. This will result in freedom and security. You can have the freedom to enjoy life and have fun as a teenager. You can be secure because he loves you and will meet every need you have.

You don't have to spend all your waking hours chasing guys. Guys are attracted to girls who are secure. When you become secure in Christ and allow God to transform you with his miracle make-over, you will be irresistible to godly guys. You may not have a date every weekend, but when you are ready, God will give you that wonderful young man who will be God's best for you.

You will have the freedom to be yourself and not worry about pleasing others. You will have the security to go to the right places and not be influenced to go to places that are not good for you. You have the freedom to say no to drugs, alcohol, and premarital sex. Because you are secure in Christ, you will not need those things to make you feel secure. When Christ has the key to your heart, you don't have to worry about what your friends think, say, or do. You will have the freedom to dress and look the way you want, not the way your friends think you should. You will be able to stand strong and feel good inside because you know you have done the right thing. You will have the freedom to love and be loved exactly the way God planned.

Many people think Christianity is a set of rules to spoil your fun. They think being a Christian means you are not free to enjoy life.

Actually, being a Christian is exactly the opposite. Read John 8:32-36. What does verse 32 say about freedom?

_____

_____

_____

_____

What does Jesus say in verse 34 about bondage?

_____

_____

What does Jesus say in verse 36 about freedom?

_____

_____

Who is the Son?

_____

_____

When you accept Christ, he gives you true freedom.

Aren't freedom and security wonderful? You don't have to wait any longer. Look back at the first page of this chapter. Read what you wrote about freedom. Do you feel the same now? If not, how do you feel differently? ☺

_____

_____

_____

_____

## WHICH STICKY NOTE DID I WRITE MY PASSWORD ON?

Write a prayer of thanksgiving to God for the freedom he has given
you.

_____

_____

_____

_____

CoolgirlChristi: Hi! I've got this really big problem. Can you help me?

**VirtualYou77: I'll sure try. What's the problem?**

CoolgirlChristi: My best friend always tells me about her problems with other people. I found out she got mad at me, too, and said some really bad things about me online. I thought she was the only person I could trust. Now I don't have anyone! What am I gonna do?

**VirtualYou77: I'm sorry your friend hurt you. At one time or another, friends and family will disappoint you. That's just a fact of life. No one is perfect. But there is one person you can always trust. Would you like to know who it is?**

CoolgirlChristi: Cool! I can't wait to meet this person. Who is it?

# TWO

# Click Onto a Real Relationship

All it takes is a click of your computer and you can chat with a friend all the way across the world on the Internet. Cyberspace relationships develop every day. Teens are talking ... and they're doing it on the Net.

For some girls, it seems less scary to tell someone about themselves anonymously. It's really fun to meet new and interesting people. One girl built a friendship with a guy across the United States. They talked for hours at a time on the Internet. He said the coolest things and made her feel really good. She had a cyber-crush. He was the quarterback for the football team, held the record for the 400-meter run for his high school, and was absolutely a dream come true! Her guy was perfect ... until she found out that *he* was really a *group of girls from her school* playing a trick on her. What a mean and cruel joke! Talk about an embarrassing moment! Her cyber-relationship turned out not to be a real relationship at all.

Have you ever been disappointed in a relationship that did not turn out to be exactly what you thought it was? If so, explain what happened. ☺

_____

_____

_____

_____

Every girl has been disappointed over relationships in her life. Like Lauren, maybe you spent most of your day chasing your guy and, finally, he asked you out. Your dream came true. Then after you really got to know him, he was a total jerk. All your dreams and hopes were shattered. He did not meet the deep needs of your heart like you thought he would. No matter how hard you tried to tell him what you needed, he never seemed to live up to your expectations.

Wouldn't it be great to find someone who could meet the deep needs of your heart? There is one relationship that will never disappoint you. This relationship is a little bit like a cyber-relationship. You can't see this person, but you can communicate with him and have a deep, personal relationship. He will always be there when you need him. You never have to wait to get on-line. His line is never busy, and he will never play a mean, cruel joke on you. He loves you so much; he would never do anything to hurt you.

In fact, he was willing to die for you on a Roman cross 2,000 years ago. His name is Jesus Christ, the Son of the one, true God. And he wants more than anything to have a relationship with you! Isn't that an awesome thought?

When you talk with someone in a chat room, you never know if that person is telling the truth. That is one thing you never have to worry about in your relationship with Jesus.

❤ Read John 14:6 in your Bible. Copy the verse and memorize it this week. What does it say about Jesus?

_____

_____

_____

You can depend on Jesus and trust him. He has proven to be trustworthy. The Bible, God's love letter to you, has proven to be true throughout the years. People have tried to destroy it, to prove it untrue, and to argue that it doesn't apply to life in this century. They have been unsuccessful. Wouldn't it be wonderful to have a relationship with someone whom you could really trust, who would never disappoint you, and who truly loves you more than life itself? You can!

We've already realized Jesus can give you security. There are, however, some significant steps you must take in building a relationship with him. The basis for building a relationship is making the decision to do it. Before you can build a relationship with a person, you must decide with whom you want to build a relationship. Then you have to take the first step. Sometimes that is the hardest part. I think that is why cyber-relationships are easy for most people. You do not have to go up and meet the person face-to-face. Deciding to build a relationship with Jesus is just as easy. It's like **A, B, C ...**

**A**dmit you are a sinner. Read Romans 3:23. What does this verse say about sinners?

_____

_____

_____

_____

_____

_____

What does this verse say about you?

_____

_____

_____

_____

**B**elieve in your heart that Jesus died for you. Read Romans 10:9. What does this verse mean to you?

_____

_____

_____

_____

These verses emphasize you must believe with your heart. Many people believe with their head but not their heart. No human attempt or achievement can make a person right with God. Jesus did everything necessary for salvation.

**C**onfess with your mouth. Read Romans 10:10. Write this verse in your own words.

_____

_____

_____

_____

These verses also emphasize that a girl must not only believe with her heart, but also confess that Jesus is Lord.

No one can make this decision for you. Parents can make other decisions like where you go, what you wear, who you hang out with, but this is one decision that is completely yours. Just because you have gone to church all your life, or just because your parents are Christians, does not mean you are a Christian and have a relationship with Jesus. Once you have made the decision, no one can ever take it from you. Wow! That is true freedom.

Read John 16:8 in your Bible. Who is the only person who can convict you of sin?

_____

_____

_____

_____


The Holy Spirit, who is the Spirit of God, is the only person who can give you the desire to receive Jesus Christ as your Savior. But even he won't force you. It's entirely up to you.

Write your testimony in the following spaces. A testimony simply tells how you became a Christian. Just fill in the following blanks and that will be your testimony.

What was your life like before you accepted Christ? ☺

_____

_____

_____

_____

_____

How did you come to realize you needed to accept Christ? ☺

_____

_____

_____

_____

How did you accept Christ? ☺

_____

_____

_____

_____

What has your life been like since you accepted Christ? ☺

_____

_____

_____

_____

If you can't remember the time you asked Jesus Christ into your heart, would you like to make that decision today?

_____

_____

Here's how: Admit to God you are a sinner. Accept what Jesus did on the cross for you. He was willing to die to accept the punishment for your sins. Ask God to forgive you. Thank him for what he has done in your life.

The words of your prayer are not magic. It's not the prayer that saves you. It is the fact that you really mean it in your heart. True sorrow and brokenheartedness over your sin is what God wants. He does not forgive you because you deserve it. He forgives you because Jesus accepted the punishment for your sins. He loves you more than your friends do. He loves you more than your parents do. He loves you more than you can imagine. What would you like to say to him today?

_____

_____

_____

_____

_____

_____

_____

_____

If you made that decision today, welcome to freedom, security, and protection. You now have the Spirit of God living in your heart. You are a Christian. He will never leave you. He is there to guide and protect you. This is the beginning of the most important relationship you will ever have—a relationship in which you will never be disappointed. However, there is something equally important. This is the beginning of a miracle makeover in your life. This transformation will take place from the inside out. What an exciting thought!

Live4Him7: I recently became a Christian and I really want to be religious, but I don't know how. Can you help me?

**VirtualYou77: I'm really happy you became a Christian. I would love to guide you in learning how to have a relationship with Jesus. Being a Christian is really more about a relationship than religion.**

Live4Him7: Really? I never knew there was a difference. Where do we start?

**VirtualYou77: Okay, great! Let's start where any good relationship starts ...**

# THREE

# Who's in Your Chat Room?

Since this relationship with Jesus is so important, how does a girl get started and develop the kind of relationship that will give her protection, security, and freedom?

There are some significant steps you must take in building relationships. First, you must spend time with the person you want to get to know. Never talking, sharing feelings, dreams, or plans would make a pretty boring twosome. That would not be much of a relationship, would it? It's the same with Jesus. To get to know him, you must spend time with him. There are several steps you must take to develop a personal relationship with him.

## You've Got Mail!

When you have a new E-mail from someone special, do you sit in front of your computer and stare at the icon? Maybe you think, "Oh, I will save that E-mail for next week! He *is* cute, but I really don't want to know what his E-mail says."

NO! You would click as soon as you saw it. Your eyes would scan down until you saw the ending. Did he say, "I love you," or "Your friend"? You would read the E-mail because what he has to say is important to you. You want to know more about him.

God has an E-mail for you too! It's a love letter written especially for you. It's called the Bible. God's Word is full of what he thinks about you. You can get to know him and discover how he feels about you and how much he loves you. He says, "I love you" all the way from Genesis to Revelation. Read Psalm 139 and write the ways God loves you.

_____

_____

_____

_____

_____


## Every Good Book Has a Love Story

Have you ever heard the saying, "Every good book has a love story"? Let's think about it. Name your favorite book. ☺

_____

Was there a love story in the plot of the book? Maybe it was a novel about prairie days, or a novel about teens of today, but probably somewhere in the story was that special relationship between a guy and a girl. That love story kept you turning those pages!

The Bible is no different. Let's see if we can discover the love story....

In the beginning, God desired to have someone to love, to take care of, to adore, to cherish. He wanted a bride, so he created mankind to be his "beloved."

Mankind was the object of his affection—someone he could know personally and intimately. God was pure and holy. Because of his perfect nature, he could not be joined with evil. So his bride had to be pure and holy also.

Satan was originally created to be one of the heavenly beings. He was ambitious and wanted to be greater than God. He was proud and cunning and rebelled against God. Because of God's holiness, he had no choice except to drive Satan from heaven. Thus God became Satan's ultimate enemy.

He realized he could never defeat God; instead, he decided to break God's heart. Therefore, Satan "seduced" God's beloved bride, the object of his affection, the one whom God adored. God's beloved betrayed him with his worst enemy. Satan persuaded God's bride to be disobedient. Oh, it was more than just disobedience; it was a disloyalty that could be compared to "sleeping with the enemy."

Satan was more clever and cunning than we could ever imagine. He knew God was holy and just and could not be joined with evil. His awareness of God's eternal law gave him the ammunition he needed. And so, God was forced to cast his bride out of the garden. Sin separated God from mankind. His heart was broken.

God longed to have his bride back. He made the law, but mankind could not live up to the law. He provided a way to sacrifice the blood of animals for the forgiveness of sin so his bride could prove her dedication to him, but he knew reconciliation was impossible because of her sinful nature.

God knew the only way she could be saved was with the perfect lifeblood of Jesus Christ, his only Son, a part of himself. God provided a way of forgiveness that would last forever, once and for all.

He sent the ultimate sacrifice, his only Son, Jesus Christ. Jesus died on the cross to pay for the sins of his bride. He suffered for every sin from the beginning of time until the end of the age. On the cross, he became the victim and the villain. Even God seemed to turn away.

Finally, Satan thought he had revenge. Jesus was dead! God was separated from his beloved! Now God had lost everything that was precious to him.

However, Satan was wrong. Three days later, Jesus Christ arose from that dark grave of suffering. Hallelujah! Satan had lost! Death and sin were defeated. All of heaven rejoiced and applauded as if it were the ending of the greatest love story ever told, but it was only the beginning.

God would finally have his "beloved" back with him. Now his bride could love him, not because she must, but because she had a choice. God's ultimate plan was the very best!

Someday in heaven, God will look on his beautiful bride with the eyes of a bridegroom who loves his bride more than anything else. Together they will celebrate the Marriage Feast of the Lamb. He will spend eternity with her and she with him. Is that not an incredible love story? In fact, it is *the* greatest love story ever told.

Jesus used wedding imagery to depict his present and future relationship with the church. The church is not a building. The church is made up of Christians. In Mark 2:19, Jesus called himself the Bridegroom. In Revelation 19:7-9, the marriage of the Lamb occurs when Christ returns and takes the church (Christians) to heaven. The church is his bride and he is the Bridegroom. Verse 9 says, "Blessed are those who are called to the marriage supper of the Lamb." I want to be there, don't you?

Does that not make cold chills on your arms? Maybe you never realized God loves you so much. He does, and he wants to spend time with you every day. He wants to hear your beautiful voice and learn of your love for him.

God loves you so much he provided a way for you to spend time with him even before you go to heaven. It's called prayer. You can pray in your mind and he knows your thoughts. You can pray out loud and he hears you. You can write your love letters to him, and he sees and knows your thoughts before you write them.

You never have to wait to get on-line. God's line is always open. Prayer is a lot more than asking God for things. Prayer is talking to God just as you would a friend. It's your opportunity to tell him your feelings and listen to him talk to you in the quietness of your heart. He cares about every part of your life. He holds the answers to your many problems, no matter what they are. Prayer is not only asking God to do things in your life and the lives of others; it is a way to know God intimately.

Some people pray when they are in trouble. "Lord, if you will help me out of this mess, I promise I will go to Africa and be a missionary." When God answers the prayer, they forget the promise. The Bible says it is better not to make a promise than to make a promise you don't intend to keep.

Some people pray when they want something new. "Lord, please give me a new red convertible."

"Lord, I really want Eric to ask me out for a date this weekend. Just one date, Lord, that's all I want."

Does that sound familiar? How would you feel if you had a good friend who only called you up when she wanted something from you?

The main purpose of prayer is fellowship with God, and knowing his will and how you fit into it. "Lord, lead me today to know what to do. Help me make right decisions that will be pleasing to you. Keep me away from evil today. Give me a way of escape when I face temptation."

If you want to know more about praying, there are some good examples in the Bible. A good prayer to begin with is found in Matthew 6:5-15. Jesus teaches about prayer. Write Jesus' prayer and then list some things from these verses that you didn't know about prayer. ☺

_____
_____
_____
_____
_____
_____

Jesus emphasizes that big, fancy words are not important. He wants to hear straight from your heart. Jesus is not impressed when we pray to look good in front of other people. How would you feel if your guy said things about you to impress other people but he never talked directly to you from his heart? Not good, huh?

Are your prayers important to God? Let's see what the Bible says about that. Read Revelation 5:8 and write what the golden bowls of incense are.

_____
_____

Who is the Lamb?

_____

_____

_____

_____

What are the four living creatures and twenty-four elders doing with the golden bowls?

_____

_____

_____

_____

_____

_____

Where is this event happening?

_____

_____

_____

_____

Who are the saints?

_____

_____

_____

_____

_____

We see that one day in heaven, the prayers of Christians will be presented in golden bowls of incense to Jesus on his throne. Our prayers must be pretty important!

Reading the Bible and praying is important, but there is a third step that will enhance your relationship with God. When you have a major crush on a guy, you try to find out everything about him, right? You know where he lives, what he eats, what color he likes, what kind of car he drives, what he enjoys doing, where he goes on Friday nights—everything! So, logically, if you are trying to build a relationship with God, you need to find out everything about him. A good way to do that is by going to church and learning as much as you can there about him. Sunday School, discipleship, worship service, choir, and youth meetings will help you learn about God. Some girls find out where their crush goes on Friday night, and then just happen to show up. So it seems like a good idea to go where God is.

We know that God is everywhere, but because he is holy, he cannot be involved in evil. So when you choose to go places where evil is going on, it's difficult to have peace with God. He wants to be with you, even on Friday night. Do you go to places that are not honoring to God? If you do, write down the places you will choose not to go any longer. ☺

_____

_____

_____

_____

_____

It's not only important to be careful where you go, but you must also be careful with whom you hang out.

Read James 4:4 and ♥ I Corinthians 15:33. What do these verses say about the friends with whom you associate?

_____

_____

_____

_____

Do you have friends who will bring you closer to God, or do you have friends who drag you away from God? God expects us to show his love to everyone, but up-close and personal relationships should point us closer to Christ. Do you have relationships in which you need to change your level of involvement? _____

If so, what is your plan?

_____

_____

_____

_____

Jesus spent up-close and personal time with twelve men. He traveled with, ate with, lived with, shared secrets with, and laughed with these twelve men. They were his "buds," his best friends. These men were his disciples, yet Jesus still sought to show God's love to people who were not his disciples.

On the other hand, there were some people Jesus avoided

because of danger. Read Matthew 12:14-16 and 2 Timothy 2:22-26. What do these tell you about people with whom you associate? ☺

_____

_____

_____

_____

_____

Some of you reading this book may be doing so in a small group of girls with an adult leader. This group can be positive peer support for you. It can be a group like Jesus had with the twelve disciples. It's important to reach out to others for the purpose of bringing them to Christ, but it's also important to protect yourself from negative peer pressure that will ruin your life and cause you to fall away from God.

Your relationship with Jesus Christ is the most significant relationship you will ever have. Reading his love letters, listening to him, talking to him, spending time with him, learning all you can about him, and choosing friends who will encourage you to live for him will all make your relationship with Jesus deeper and more meaningful. A relationship with Jesus will continue the process of the miracle makeover in your life.

It will be easier to get to know Jesus and build a relationship with him if you have a specific plan for doing so. Many people call it a "quiet time" or "devotional." Following is a Quiet Time Guide to help you. Use this guide every day, and soon you will develop a life-long habit.

## Quiet Time Guide

1. *Choose a time.* Make an appointment with God. Choose the same time every day if possible. Before long you will form a habit.

2. *Choose a place.* The place should be a quiet place with few distractions. You may choose a favorite spot outside if the weather permits. You may choose your room or other quiet place in your home. Most teens can do many things at the same time such as listen to the radio, watch TV, and talk on the Internet while studying, but it is important to focus totally on God during this time.

3. *Bring your Bible, a pen, paper, and a devotional guide.* Choose a translation of the Bible that is easy for you to understand. There are many devotional guides from which to choose. *EC (Essential Connection),* published by LifeWay, and *Devo'Zine,* published by The Upper Room, are two good ones. Christian bookstores carry many excellent devotional books also.

4. *Begin your quiet time with a short prayer.* Ask God to speak to you and help you understand what you read. Read your devotional guide and then read the scripture indicated. The Bible is actually God's love letter to you!

5. *Write the points in the scripture.* Write how God is speaking to you about what you have read.

6. *Close with prayer.* Talk to God just as you would if he were sitting with you as a friend. (He actually is your Friend!) You may like to write your prayers to God. When God answers a specific prayer, go back and check it off with a red pen. This will help you see how many times God answers your prayers.

Having a daily quiet time may be difficult at first, but before long you will begin to look forward to your time alone with God. It will be a cool time where God will show you things in your life you need to change or things you need to begin doing. God is more interested in your heart than in what you do for him! He will change your heart. You will begin to notice a difference in your attitude and how you think about your life. God loves you so much! He wants to spend time with you every day!

## INSTANT MESSAGE

Nlove4ever: I need your help. I have this great boyfriend! He is totally cool, but I am confused right now. He really wants me to have sex with him, but my friends tell me I shouldn't. They just don't understand how much I love him. I don't want my friends to think I'm terrible, but I don't want to lose my boyfriend either. What should I do?

**VirtualYou77: Sounds like you have a big decision to make. Let's weigh this situation out. First, let's discuss why it would be okay to have sex. Then, we can discuss why it might not be a good idea. Maybe that will help you make your decision.**

Nlove4ever: Okay, that's cool. Sounds like you are not trying to tell me what to do.... I like it when adults tell me the pros and cons and let me make my own decisions.

**VirtualYou77: Yeah, I like to teach teens how to make wise decisions for themselves. One day soon, you'll be out on your own and have to make decisions yourself. If you learn now, you'll be in great shape when you get out on your own.**

Nlove4ever: Ur the bomb! Where do we start?

# FOUR

# Has Your Purity Code Been Hacked? (Part 1)

Did you know there are professional hackers: people whose job is to break the code on other people's computers to get vital information? Unfortunately, there are "professional purity hackers" also. What is your purity code? Where did it come from? How do you decide whether you will have sex before marriage or not? How do you decide what you put into your mind or body? How do you know right from wrong? How do you choose right? How do you protect your purity code?

Let's see what Jesus has to say about purity. Read Matthew 15:16-20. According to Jesus, where does impurity come from?

_____

_____

_____

_____

List the impure things that Jesus says come from the heart.

_____

_____

_____

_____

_____

When a girl strives for purity in her heart, what do you think the results will be?

_____

_____

_____

Many people try to teach abstinence or "just say no" to teenagers. They tell teens not to have sex before marriage, not to drink alcohol, and not to use drugs. Most of the time, abstinence programs don't really work that well. Abstinence programs sometimes use condoms and other methods of birth control for backup when their program fails. They offer support groups for teens who are pregnant or addicted to drugs and alcohol when the "just say no" program fails. Let's think about this more....

What happens inside your mind when someone tells you not to do something?

_____

_____

_____

_____

If you are like most people, it causes you to want it more. People are naturally rebellious. Abstinence programs tell you, "Don't have sex, don't drink alcohol, and don't use drugs."

On the other hand, when you are given a goal to strive for, it doesn't make you feel rebellious. Setting up a goal of purity in your heart and mind will result in pure thoughts, words, and actions. When you set up a goal of purity in your life, abstinence will be a result! Once you have set up a goal of purity, how do you protect it? Let's see if we can get the big picture.

What many guys want and what a girl needs are not necessarily the same thing! My husband speaks to youth groups often and sometimes has the opportunity to speak to groups of guys. He always gets a big round of applause when he makes this statement, "Guys are turned on by three things: (1) What they see, (2) What they see, and (3) What they see." Guys tend to agree.

During the teen years, many guys are like one big hormone walking around in tennis shoes. Many guys eat, sleep, and breathe sex. In the world we live in today, sex is the hook of many commercials, TV programs, magazine covers, movies, books, and Internet sites. It's hard for guys or girls to go through the day without thinking of sexual things either consciously or subconsciously. Sex is thrown at you in many different ways. Even fashion magazines for teenage girls and young women are full of ideas on dressing sexy, catching a guy by having sex, and enhancing your sex life. It's hard to know right from wrong.

The truth is, guys have a hard time controlling sexual thoughts and actions, and sometimes girls make it even harder for them. God created guys to be physical beings. That's why guys are so interested in physical activities such as sports and sex. God created girls to be more emotional beings. That's why we like warm fuzzies, affection, romance, and love stories. Don't get me wrong—girls like sex, too. But there is one important element that has to happen before a girl (most girls) feels comfortable giving her body to a guy. She must give her heart and emotions first. That's not necessarily true with a guy. Many guys can have sex with a girl and not feel the slightest emotional connection in their hearts.

Some guys think only of their own selfish desires and make it their business to hack your purity code. They figure out where girls are weak and they crack the code with "I love you's," flowers, romance, and whatever else it takes. Some girls think of their own selfish desires to be loved and have a boyfriend. They are willing to do whatever it takes to hook up with a guy. That sets up an explosive situation, and before you know it, "BAM!" it's over.

So why should you wait? Is it really wrong to have sex if you really love him? Let's figure it out together.

Name the reasons you think it would be okay to have sex before marriage. (I know that's not a question you are normally asked, but this is important!) Just think about it. ☺

_____

_____

_____

_____

Now, name the reasons you think it's not okay to have sex before marriage. ☺

_____

_____

_____

_____

Why would I ask you two such questions? When, where, and why you have sex, and with whom are decisions only you can make for yourself. Some parents have set a good example and some parents haven't. Maybe your parents tell you not to have sex outside of marriage, or your youth minister tells you not to. Your friends can try to influence you to have sex or not to have sex. But the bottom line is, it's your decision. You need to understand both sides in order to make a wise choice for your life. Let's go on....

### Light My Fire

Have you ever lit a match and put it in the fireplace on a cold winter evening? Soon you had a warm cozy fire. You curled up with a good book and the light of the fire danced on the pages as you read. The crackling of the fire soothed you with a calm, peaceful feeling. You sipped hot chocolate as you read—what a wonderful thought. Sounds like a perfect evening!

On the other hand, have you ever lit a match and held it close to your clothes? Soon you would be warm, but not cozy. The crackling sound would be the same, but it would not give you a cozy, peaceful feeling. That's a pretty scary thought!

The contrast of these two fires is the same as comparing sex in marriage and sex outside of marriage. In the first scenario, the fire is used for its purpose and it's very good. In the second scenario, the fire is used outside its purpose, and it's deadly.

God created sex, and he did a very good job! But he had a specific purpose in mind. The sexual relationship between a husband and wife is the deepest human relationship possible. This relationship joins a man and woman together as one. The purpose for sexual intercourse is to provide the union and closeness that God planned for one woman and one man for a lifetime, and for bearing children. Sex inside the marriage relationship is a beautiful, wonderful union. Sex outside the marriage relationship is like a deadly fire that will devastate and destroy lives. You may find pleasure for a moment, but soon the consequences come and you wish you had never gone there.

## The Truth About Consequences

Every decision in life has consequences. Some are good. Some are bad. Some you live with the rest of your life, and some you don't. Let's talk about some of the consequences when trying to decide if you want to have sex before marriage or not. There are three major areas affected when you make the decision to have sex before marriage: your body, your mind, and your soul. Let's look at one girl's situation.

Shannon was the president of her youth group at church. She was a godly young teen who made wise choices most of the time; however, she made one decision that changed her life forever. There was a guy at school who was the crush of every red-blooded American girl with whom he came in contact. Shannon was no different. She first noticed Zack while she was at cheerleading practice one day. He was awesome—quarterback of the football team, muscular, tall, dark, and handsome. His eyes seemed to look straight through you, and he knew just the right thing to say at the right time.

It didn't take him long to hook up with Shannon since she was a very beautiful girl. She invited him to come to church with her.

He resisted for a few weeks, but finally gave in to her. Shannon felt in her heart she could influence Zack to become a Christian. Her feelings began to grow for him.

It first started with little kisses and hugs, but each time they were together their passion grew. Each time they went a little bit further, but Shannon stopped him before things got out of hand. Shannon asked forgiveness in her quiet times with the Lord and promised never to do it again. However, it seemed as though this guy had some kind of power over her that was terribly hard to resist.

Then one night, it happened. It couldn't be reversed. She was no longer a virgin. Somehow, the romance, the passion, the love she had felt, was zapped in a few minutes' time. She felt sick. Her mind raced, "What have I done?" "How could I let this happen?"

The coldness in Zack's eyes was the most sickening to her. As he pulled in front of her house to drop her off, he said with a coldness that sent chills up and down her spine, "I guess I just blew your Christianity all to pieces, huh?" His passionate, caring attitude had turned to hate. The next week at school when they passed in the hall, his eyes glared straight ahead. It was as if she had never existed. She didn't hear from him after that.

Shannon talked with her youth minister the next week. He told her of God's love and forgiveness even though she had messed up. Shannon prayed and asked God to forgive her. Her life seemed to be going in the right direction after that. She had learned a valuable lesson. One that she would never forget!

Several months later she was sitting at lunch with her friends. She overheard a conversation at the table beside her.

"I can't believe it! He seemed so nice."

"Yeah, and he looked so clean. When did he find out?"

"I think he's known for a good while and just didn't tell anyone."

"You're kidding! Will he still be able to come to school? Man, what a bummer!"

Shannon was curious by this time, but she really tried not to get involved in gossip. Then it was clear.

"Are you kidding? Zack has AIDS!"

Shannon's food stuck in her throat. She couldn't swallow. Tears began to sting her eyes as she gathered her books, leaving her lunch tray on the table.

Unfortunately, Shannon lived with the consequences of her decision the rest of her short life.

## Your Body

Just twenty years ago, sex outside of a faithful, monogamous marriage ran the risk of gonorrhea, syphilis, and pregnancy. (Faithful means you never have had or will have sex with anyone else. Monogamous means you will be married to that one person for a lifetime.) When you have "unprotected sex" (marriage is the only true protection!) all of those diseases are still a risk in this new century, but there is an added risk. Today, sex outside of marriage spells DEATH for many. The American Association for World Health has recently released new statistics revealing the following:

Every day, more than 7,000 people between the ages of 15 and 24 are infected with HIV worldwide. Even scarier? Only one in four sexually active teens in the United States has ever been tested for HIV.

From this information, we see the number of teens who have the virus that causes AIDS is likely to be a tremendously high number. They just don't know it yet.

The Center for Disease Control and the Federal Drug Administration answer frequently asked questions. I think you might find some of those questions interesting or maybe even shocking:

Q) Can I get HIV from performing oral sex or having oral sex performed on me?

A) Yes, it is possible to become infected with HIV through performing oral sex. Blood, semen, pre-seminal fluid, and vaginal fluid all may contain the virus cells. Cells in the lining of the mouth may carry HIV into the lymph nodes or bloodstream.

Q) Do condoms eliminate the risk of pregnancy and getting HIV or other STDs (sexually transmitted diseases)?

A) No, there is no absolute guarantee that condoms will entirely eliminate the risk of getting pregnant, HIV, or other STDs.

Q) Can I get HIV from open-mouth kissing?

A) Prolonged open-mouth kissing could damage the mouth and lips and allow HIV to pass from an infected person to a partner and then enter the body through cuts or sores in the mouth. Because of the possible risk, the Center for Disease Control advises against open-mouth kissing with an infected partner.

How do you know if a guy is infected or not? If he has ever had sex, the possibility is there. How do you know if he has had sex or not? You must rely on his answer. Can you trust him? Knowing if you can trust a person takes a long time. Is your life worth a moment's pleasure?

The AIDS epidemic is not about to disappear any time soon. There is no cure. Actually, we see that sex outside of a faithful monogamous marriage can be even deadlier than lighting a match and holding it next to your clothes. Why? The fire can be extinguished. AIDS cannot!

The comforting thought about these statistics is this: When you strive for a life of purity, abstinence will be a result. *When two uninfected people, who have had no other sex partners besides each other, marry and remain faithful to each other for a lifetime, their lives and hearts will be protected.*

Not only can the threat of STDs affect your body, but getting pregnant is also a big risk. In the last couple of years there has been a "safe sex" campaign to encourage teens to use condoms. We saw in the previous questions that condoms are not approved by the FDA (Federal Drug Administration) as an absolutely effective method of birth control. Why? Because condoms cannot be trusted to work! There is some percentage of failure to prevent STDs and failure to prevent pregnancy, plus a 100 percent failure to prevent emotional trauma, which is the next area we will talk about.

**Your Mind**

I saw a terribly sad situation not long ago. I was in a restaurant and saw a teenage boy who had been badly burned. The scars were horrendous. He had a large hat pulled down as far as he could around his head and face. The hat really didn't hide the unsightly scars. He kept his head down and never looked face-to-face with anyone. My mind was spinning as I wondered what had happened, probably in minutes, to change his whole life so drastically.

Evidently, it was a fire of some kind that left him not only with terrible scars on his body but also terrible scars and anguish in his mind. How angry and bitter he looked. How embarrassed and lonely he seemed.

The deadly fire of sex outside marriage leaves scars just as devastating, not only physically but also emotionally. Many teen mothers experience the bitterness and anger of missing out on the fun of their teenage years, simply because there was a child, a human life, for whom they were responsible. Some teenage mothers work long hours, go to school at night to get their GED, and still have the responsibility of meeting the needs of their child. Then there is the loneliness of being the odd man out when everyone else is dating, going to the prom, football games, and just hanging out together.

Most girls who have sex before marriage go through the emotional embarrassment of thinking *everyone* knows what she did last night. Her relationship changes with her parents and friends. She is not as free and open with them. Her conversations are guarded because she doesn't want to give away her secret.

There is also a hidden consequence that sometimes pops up years later. If you have sex and then later marry the guy, thoughts begin to run through your head. "If he didn't show self-control with me before marriage, is he showing self-control with his secretary at work today? Did he marry me because he really wanted to, or just because we had already had sex?" God wants to prevent this kind of emotional hurt and pain in your life. His Word is full of warnings against sexual impurity.

Look in the back of your Bible at the concordance and see how many verses you can find related to sex, sexual purity, sexual immorality, sexual intimacy, etc.

List each scripture reference and a short summary of the verse.

_____

_____

_____

_____

_____

_____

_____

_____

_____

_____

_____

_____

_____

_____

_____

_____

_____

_____

_____

There are many verses related to sexual purity and God's plan for sexual relationships in the Bible. If there are this many verses, do you think God must think it's a pretty important topic to know about? Ask God to show you some things about sexual purity you never knew about before.

_____

_____

_____

_____

_____

_____

## Your Spirit

When a little kid takes cookies from the cookie jar before dinner, most of the time he will hide from his mother to eat them. He doesn't want her to know he has been disobedient. When we are involved in sexual sin, we tend to try to hide from God. Sin affects your relationship with God. When you have sin in your life, it's hard to approach God every morning in your quiet time, or talk to him freely about things going on in your life.

Since God is perfect and holy in every way, he cannot be joined with impurity. The Holy Spirit (the Spirit of God) lives inside you when you become a Christian. When you are involved in sexual sin, the Holy Spirit is grieved and seems distant, leaving you spiritually depressed.

One girl who was involved in sexual sin described it this way: "When I was involved in sex, it felt like I was hovering over watching. I couldn't believe what I saw myself doing."

Ephesians 4:30a says, "Do not grieve the Holy Spirit of God." When a child of God is involved in sin, the Holy Spirit is grieved and pulls back a bit. He never leaves you, but he can't be involved in sin. It's kind of as if he is hovering over watching. The Spirit of God is grieved when we choose to sin.

Sexual sin not only affects your relationship with God, but it affects your relationship with others—parents, friends, Christians, and non-Christians. It's hard to be a Christian influence on others when they know you have sin in your life. When you are sexually involved on a date, it's easy to come home and go straight to your room to avoid talking with your parents or family. Thoughts go through your mind—*Maybe they can look at me and tell what I've been doing. What if I slip up and say something to give away my secret?*

If you are trying to influence a guy to become a Christian and you end up having sex with him, what kind of Christian influence do you think you can have? You may be like Shannon. Zack "blew her Christianity all to pieces."

# Has Your Purity Code Been Hacked? (Part 2)

Just as computers have security zones to protect information on the Internet, God has security zones to protect your purity. Why do you think God's rules are so specific about sex outside of marriage? Do you think he wants to spoil your fun? Do you think he wants to make you miserable? Write your thoughts in this space.☺

_____

_____

_____

_____

_____

Read Ephesians 6:14b. The verses surrounding this verse talk about the armor of God. The armor is compared to the armor that soldiers wore in battle centuries ago. Each piece of the armor represents God's way of protecting his children. This particular verse talks about the breastplate of righteousness. The breastplate is the piece of armor soldiers used to protect vital organs during battle. The breastplate was designed mainly to protect the heart.

Righteousness means living in obedience to God, making right choices, avoiding sin, and being pure and holy. What do you think will happen when you live a righteous life? ☺

_____

_____

_____

_____

_____

God loves you so much he wants to protect you from pain and heartache. He knows being involved in sex outside of marriage will cause you unnecessary heartache and pain. He knows if you live a righteous life, your heart will be protected from the consequences of personal sin. So God's rules protect you from self-inflicted hurt and pain.

## The Virtual Kiss-Off

The government and large companies hire people to guard against hackers. They spend large amounts of money to protect their computer information from falling into the wrong hands. Girls need to guard against purity hackers too! How is that possible? Do you put yourself in a bubble until you get married? Do you stay home every weekend and never go out on dates? No! God wants you to go out, have fun, and enjoy being a teenager! But there are a few steps you can take to guard your purity.

Several years ago a popular movie came out about a young woman who had fallen prey to prostitution. She hated having sex with men she did not know, but continued prostitution to survive financially. One night a rich, good-looking executive picked her up on the street corner and hired her for two weeks. She had one rule. No kissing. Why would this young woman do anything her customer wanted except kiss?

Evidently, she knew about the heartstrings that are attached to her lips. Kissing affects a girl's heart and emotions, but it affects a guy's physical state. Remember at the beginning of this chapter we talked about a girl giving her heart before giving her body. Prostitutes give their bodies, but guard their hearts to prevent the emotional pain when the guy leaves money beside the bed and walks out.

Kissing affects every girl the same. What would happen if you stopped kissing every guy you like? Would the world come to an end? Probably not, but let's think about this more. Write in the space exactly what a kiss means to you. ☺

_____

_____

_____

_____


Most girls say things like, "He loves me. He thinks I'm special. He cares about me. He likes me. He thinks I'm pretty." Sometimes girls say they feel obligated to kiss a guy or feel afraid he won't like them if they say no.

I did an experiment and asked a few guys what a kiss means to them. The number one answer was "conquest" and "victory." Are you shocked? Many girls don't realize the different make-up of guys and girls. When the Holy Spirit does not control our lives, our selfish nature will take over.

I once heard someone say, "Guys are microwaves, girls are crockpots." Think about kissing as the start button on a microwave for a guy. Do you really want to cook that quickly? Most girls prefer the slower "crockpot" style, but they find the meal is already burned before they can blink an eye. Many girls do not realize how strongly kissing affects a guy sexually, since most girls are affected more emotionally when kissing. The relationship will progress too quickly sexually and emotionally when heavy kissing occurs.

Another question to help you make your decision about kissing is this: "To whom do your kisses belong?" When you really think about it, your body, your kisses, and your gift of sex really belong to your husband. I know it's hard to think about your husband when you are only a teenager, but it's important to think about the future. When you give your kisses away freely, you are really giving something that is not yours to give. It would be a shame to know you wasted your kisses to thank a guy for a hamburger and Coke. It's scary to think what you would have to give for a steak dinner!

Is there another way to thank a guy for a wonderful evening out or a meal? Write your thoughts. ☺

_____

_____

_____

_____

_____

_____

_____

When your kisses are given freely, it becomes much easier to give your heart as a result and much harder to guard your purity. It's difficult to think objectively. Instead of making decisions based on good sense, a girl tends to make decisions based on her feelings. Many times it is dangerous to trust your feelings. Saving your kisses or giving them sparingly is a decision only you can make, but it's one that will help you guard your heart and purity in the end.

## What Does "I Love You" Mean?

Has a guy ever whispered, "I love you," in your ear? Every girl dreams of someone special who will love and adore her for a lifetime. When a guy whispers, "I love you," what does it mean to you? ☺

_____

_____

_____

_____

_____

_____

_____

In a survey, I asked several guys (Christian and non-Christian) this question: What do you mean when you say, "I love you," to a girl? The answers were quite interesting.

One boy said, "Well, it means I love you as much as I can at this point in my life." When I questioned him further he said, "At my age (18 years old), I don't really understand what love really means. So it means, I like her a lot, but I'm not really in love with her."

Another guy said, "It means I really like to be with her." When asked if he told more than one girl at a time that he loved her, his answer was, "Oh, yes, lots of times."

I did another survey and asked older men to look back on their younger years and determine what "I love you" meant to them as a teenager. Most of them agreed that it was a manipulative statement to get a girl to make out with them or to have sex. Most agreed that love means something totally different to them now.

When asking teenage girls the same question, the answers were quite different. They said things like, "It means I am special to him. It means we have a special relationship." So you see that "I love you" means something totally different to teenage guys than it means to teenage girls.

When a guy says, "I love you," that affects your heart. It's important to guard your heart against "falling in love" with every guy who says, "I love you." When a girl falls in love, it's easier to compromise her sexual purity.

## Don't Call the Lion "Kitty, Kitty"

It is not only wise to give your kisses sparingly, and to save your "I love you's" for the right person to guard your purity, but it is also important to avoid temptation. A popular TV program, *World's Amazing Videos,* once aired an incredible home video. The video showed several boys petting a lion that appeared tame. Evidently it was a pet belonging to one of the boys. However, without warning, the lion let out a deafening roar, his head snapped around, and he fiercely attacked one of the boys. The boy's shoulder was completely engulfed in the lion's powerful jaws. His body was slapped back and forth like a rag doll. The other boys tried desperately to pull their friend from the lion's mouth. After several minutes, they were able to free his mangled body from impending death. The boy survived! One arm was completely amputated, and he will live with terrible scars the rest of his life. It was a miracle the boy was not killed!

❤ Read 1 Peter 5:8-9. With what do these verses compare the devil?

_____

_____

Many times the devil will try to tempt you with sexual activity. He will feed you the lie that if you don't "go all the way," it's not really sex. The devil will try to convince you that if you are really in love, it's okay. He will tell you that looking at pornography on the Internet or watching sexual acts in the movies does not affect how you think, feel, and act. He will feed you the lie that oral sex is "not really sex." He will lie to you about your sexual involvement the same as he lied to Eve in the garden.

Satan's ultimate goal is to destroy you physically, emotionally, and spiritually. If he can't destroy you, he will settle for mangling your life.

In verse 9, the Bible commands us to resist the devil; yet instead of resisting him, we "pet" him like the boys petted the lion. We see how close and friendly we can get to the temptation. We flirt with temptation and play with it.

It's the same as approaching a roaring lion and saying in an innocent voice, "Here, Kitty, Kitty." Now, wouldn't that be ridiculous? It's just as ridiculous to play with sexual temptation. Things may go along fine for awhile. You think you are getting away with it. You think no one will find out. You "pet that lion" and he is tame and quiet, but when you least expect it, the lion of pregnancy will pounce. When you least expect it, the lion of AIDS will pounce. When you least expect it, the lion of hepatitis or HIV pounces.

Sooner or later the lion will pounce. Sometimes the lion pounces and you are maimed; sometimes he pounces and you are dead. You may live through it or you may not. But just as the boy will live with his scars from the attack of the lion, you will live the rest of your life with the scars of sexual sin. God will forgive you, but the consequences remain.

When setting standards for dating, it is helpful to write them down on paper or in a journal. This will help you avoid temptation. One girl wisely added the following into her list of standards:

- I will not be alone in my house, his house, in my bedroom, or in a parked car with any guy I choose to date.
- I will not lie down with any guy I choose to date.
- I will not watch movies that have strong sexual content with any guy I choose to date.
- I will not look at Internet sites that have sexual content with a guy I choose to date.
- I will not dress in any way to seduce a guy sexually.

Setting standards and sticking to them is a necessary part of avoiding temptation. We will talk more about setting standards in Chapter Five.

Can you name the three ways to guard your purity? ☺

1. _____
2. _____
3. _____

There are three categories of girls reading this book. Only you can decide which category you fit.

*Category One:* This girl has accepted Christ as her personal Lord and Savior. She does her very best to live a life of obedience. When temptation comes, she turns around and runs as fast as she can. She surrounds herself with friends who build her up and point her to Christ.

If you fit into this category, my challenge to you today is to stay on the alert. Keep your faith in God strong. Don't give the devil any opportunity to ruin your life. Never let your guard down.

*Category Two:* This girl claims to be a Christian but is still trying to pet the lion. She calls him "Kitty, Kitty" and somehow thinks he will never pounce. She plays the game and straddles the fence. She comes to church and claims to be a Christian but goes out on the weekends and is involved in sin. Read Revelation 3:16 and write the verse.

_____

_____

_____

_____

This verse says clearly that this kind of person literally makes God sick. Because she is neither hot nor cold, he will spit her out of his mouth. The New King James Version uses the word *vomit.* That's pretty strong language. This means that you must be for God or against him. You can't play the middle. That's the bottom line.

If you find yourself in this category, my challenge to you is to fall on your knees before your Heavenly Father and ask forgiveness. Accept him into your heart and life. Begin spending time with him every day, reading the Bible and praying. Ask him to show you the right choices to make. Ask him to give you godly friends to help support you. Ask him to help you set standards and stick to them. Fall passionately in love with him and be completely sold out.

*Category Three:* This girl has never accepted Christ as Savior. The lion is chasing her and she is running for her life but literally does not know which way to turn.

If you have never accepted Christ into your heart and life, my challenge to you is to turn to him right now. He wants to help you. He wants to save you from the dangers of the devil. He wants to forgive you of your sins and help you live a life of purity, godliness, and safety.

Only you can decide in which category you are at this point in your life. Be honest with yourself and God. Write your thoughts to God and allow him to work in your life today.

_____

_____

_____

_____

_____

_____

_____

_____

_____

_____

_____

_____

_____

## Is It Ever Too Late?

Maybe you have already blown it. Many girls reading this book will already feel the terrible guilt of sexual impurity and have already suffered many of the consequences discussed in this chapter. Where do you go now? What do you do? Is your life doomed? NO! NO! A thousands times NO!

God loves you! He wants you to be his child. He wants to forgive you! Read 1 John 1:9 and write this promise from God.

_____

_____

_____

_____

There is nothing you can do that will cause God not to love you. If you confess your sins (agree with God that you are wrong), then he will be faithful to forgive your sins. Read 2 Corinthians 5:17 and write God's promise to you.

God will forgive you. He will give you a new life. Sometimes the consequences of our sins cannot be taken away, but we can use those things in life to help other people.

## Sexual Abuse and Incest

Many girls have been involved sexually against their will when they were little or even now as a teenager. When someone forces you to be involved sexually, that is called sexual abuse. When a family member forces you to have sex, that is called incest. God never wants his children to suffer from abuse or incest. Often sexual abuse and incest cause the victim to feel guilty. God never holds the victim responsible. If someone has forced you to be involved sexually, God does not hold you accountable for that. Some girls have been raped or molested and have become pregnant. Some girls have been raped or molested and have gotten sexually transmitted diseases. God never intended for his precious children to suffer the consequences of sin in that way. Your pain is a result of the other person's sin. God holds that person responsible. He sees you as pure and precious. He knows your pain. He never wanted you to experience that pain. From the beginning, God never intended his children to suffer. Satan came in, and his intent is to cause heartache, pain, and suffering.

If you are suffering from sexual abuse or incest that is going on at the present time, it is important for you to tell a responsible adult whom you trust, so you can be protected. God wants you to be safe from abuse of any kind. Don't wait. Get help for yourself today.

If you were abused, raped, or molested in the past, it is still important to tell someone you trust. A responsible adult can help you find someone to counsel you and help you work through the pain and suffering you are experiencing. Don't put it off any longer. Get help today!

## Where Do I Go From Here?

It's easy to recognize someone who has experienced pain and sorrow from the consequences of sin and is now forgiven. That person takes time to help someone in need. That person is passionate about telling others what Jesus can do in their lives. God wants to use your life, your past experiences, and your testimony for his glory. God has an incredible plan for your life! Stay close to him, read his Word, and pray every day, so you will know how he wants to use you for his kingdom.

Write your prayer to God asking him to forgive you for any impurity in your heart or life. Be specific. If you need to use codes, that's okay. God knows everything, even the codes you make up.

_____

_____

_____

_____

_____

At the beginning of this chapter, you named reasons to have sex and not to have sex outside of marriage. Look back at your answers. Do you feel the same now? If not, how is it different? ☺

_____

_____

_____

_____

_____

_____

Write a prayer to God asking him to help you know truth and apply it to your life. Do you need to set a goal of purity in your heart and life? Purity means you are saving any kind of sexual relationship for the man you will marry someday. Tell God whatever decision you have made in your life as a result of what you have learned.

_____

_____

_____

_____

_____

_____

_____

_____

_____

_____

_____

_____

_____

_____

_____

_____

_____

_____

_____

_____

## INSTANT MESSAGE

**Confused4now2:** I'll get straight to the point. I'm a Christian. There's a really cool guy at school. He asked me out, but he's not a Christian. My parents tell me I should date only Christian guys. I know I can be a good influence on him, but they won't listen to me.

**VirtualYou77:** Sounds like you really want to help others know Christ. That's a great quality to have. Let's think about this more. Maybe we can figure out why your parents feel the way they do.

**Confused4now2:** They usually say, "Because I said so." I really need to know why!

**VirtualYou77:** Sounds like you're ready to get down to business.

**Confused4now2:** I am. I hope you can help me. I'm afraid he will lose interest if I put him off too long.

**VirtualYou77:** Okay, let's get busy!

# FIVE

# Cracking the Code on Guys

Does the prospect of ever having a love relationship with a guy seem pretty bleak at this point? Don't give up! There is hope! You don't have to put yourself in a bubble and avoid guys until you are an adult. You do, however, want the best God has to offer in your future husband.

In order to get the best, you must crack the code on guys. How do you figure out who they are and what they are thinking? How do you know if a particular guy would make a good husband? How do you know if the guy you are dating is the one God has chosen for you? We will attempt to crack the code together.

List the characteristics you would like your future husband to have. Remember, you will live with this person for the rest of your life! Try to focus on inward character, not physical characteristics. ☺

_____

_____

_____

_____

_____

_____

Do these characteristics make up a godly guy? If you are like most other girls, they do! Most girls want to marry a man who will be a loving husband and father, faithful and loyal, caring and under-standing, patient and kind, pleasant and personable. It helps if he is willing to work and support the family, and is willing to take care of himself by eating healthily, not using drugs or alcohol, smoking, or becoming involved in other addictions. It's really hard for a guy to exemplify these characteristics without God's help. A godly guy will pursue the things of God, study the Word of God, tell others, and be involved and supportive of the church. When a person lives his life fully devoted to Christ, then he will show godly characteristics in all areas of his life.

## Becoming a Godly Guy Magnet

The next question is tremendously important! What kind of wife do you think a godly man wants to marry? ☺

_____

_____

_____

_____

_____

Name the characteristics a godly guy would want in his wife. Again, focus on inward character, not physical characteristics.☺

_____

_____

_____

_____

_____

_____

Think about yesterday. Write down what you did from the time you got up until you went to bed. Estimate how much time you spent on each activity. Try to include everything you did such as brushing your teeth, combing your hair, what you did between classes at school, what you did between the times you left school and arrived home, etc.

_____

_____

_____

_____

_____

_____

_____

_____

Now add up how much time you spent in primping for your guy, thinking about him, going where he was, and talking about him to carefully selected friends.

_____

_____

_____

_____

_____

How much time did you spend in developing your godly character?

_____

_____

_____

Taking care of yourself and looking nice is important, but godly character is irresistible to a godly guy. Do you want to be a godly guy magnet? Then spend your time developing your godly character. You may not have a date every night of the week, but you will end up attracting God's best in the end. It will be worth the wait!

## Setting Standards for Dating

Setting standards or rules for dating is an important step in making sure you protect your heart and experience healthy dating relationships. The story of one girl is a perfect example.

Before beginning to date, her parents asked her to write down a list of dating standards. She wrote as many as she could think of and then narrowed it down to a reasonable number that covered the important issues. She sat down with her parents and asked for their advice. They finally came up with an acceptable list of dating standards. She wrote the list, decorated it, put it in a frame, and hung it up in her room where she could see it every day. When a guy asked her to go out on a date, she always measured him against her standards. If he didn't match up, she wouldn't go out with him. If she didn't know him well enough, she would try to get to know him better before agreeing to go on a date.

Write below a few standards or rules you should consider before accepting a date with a guy.

_____

_____

_____

CRACKING THE CODE ON GUYS

You can probably name the kind of guy you would *not* want to marry. But how do you know if the guy you like is one of those guys? How does a girl really get to know a guy? Name specific ways you can get to know a guy. ☺

_____

_____

_____

_____

_____

_____

Your first response may have been something like this:

- "communicating with him"
- "spending time with him"
- "asking him questions about who he is and what he likes"
- "telling him what I like and making sure we have something in common"

Sounds pretty logical, but let's think this over carefully. At a youth group meeting one night, Ashley met a seemingly awesome young man, Kirk. He was visiting the youth group with his cousin and lived in a nearby area of town. The attraction was instant. You know that feeling—when you feel that there's no one else in the room except *him*. You fear the thud of your heart will expose your weakness every time he looks your way. His eyes penetrate the depths of your heart, and he seems to know he is irresistible.

As he walked over and asked if the seat beside her was taken, a million thoughts flashed through her mind in a matter of seconds. "Will he see the zit on my chin? Did I remember to use my deodorant? Does my hair look okay? Will I say something stupid?" The minute he sat down, her anxiety began to fade. They began to talk, and it was amazing how much they had in common. Everything she said, he replied, "Cool! Me too!" Their values were the same, their likes and dislikes were the same. They even liked the same color!

She left that night feeling he was the one God had made just for her. They did everything together—just the two of them. Ashley lost contact with most of her friends. She missed going out as a group and having fun, but Kirk preferred to be alone. After all, he pointed out, they were perfect for each other. He claimed to be a Christian, but felt he could worship God in nature better than he could in church. He was totally the most romantic boy she had ever known. He planned incredible dates with candlelight, flowers, and picnics in the park. They took long walks on the beach and talked for hours on the phone. He was perfect!

Ashley's parents voiced their concern many times about this young man. Kirk always blew the horn and picked Ashley up at the curb. He made it known he didn't care to talk with her parents. Her friends even tried to talk to her, but she ignored their warnings for a long time.

Finally, they harassed her so much she decided to prove to them he was as wonderful as she thought he was. She invited him to the church family cookout on the Fourth of July. The fireworks were not the only things that exploded that night. He argued with her little brother and sister over where to sit at the table. He was rude to her friends. He refused to eat the food because it wasn't cooked to his taste. He was rude to her mom and dad, and to top it off, he burped really loud during the prayer.

That evening, he was a different person than she had seen before. When it was finally time for him to go home, he told her it was all her parents' fault that the evening had been such a flop. He said they were just like his parents—too bossy! He was so angry he ended up pushing her into the wall and squeezing her arms until they turned blue. She was flabbergasted! How could he be so wonderful when they were alone and be such a jerk when they were with her family and friends?

It bothered her at first, but after a day or so she began to see his side. She hid the bruises from her family to protect him. She loved him so much; it was hard to listen to her family and friends.

What are your thoughts about this situation? Write down the "red flags" Ashley should have noticed. ☺

_____

_____

_____

_____

_____

Why do you think it was hard for Ashley to see the weaknesses in Kirk's character?

_____

_____

_____

_____

_____

Have you ever heard the old saying, "Love is blind"? It's partly true. When you give your heart and emotions to a guy, it is easy to overlook his faults. That's why it is important to get to know him before giving your heart to him.

Many girls think getting to know a guy is sitting and talking one-on-one for hours; however, there is a danger involved. Any guy can say, "Cool! Me too!" But is it really true? (Some girls have been guilty of this, too!) Sometimes guys want you to like them so much they will try to become what you want them to be. They can keep up the masquerade for a short time, especially when they are talking one-on-one with you.

How does a girl get to really know a guy? A proven method is to watch him with other people. Ask yourself the following character questions:

1. How does he interact with guys his own age? Does he get along with other people well?

2. How does he interact with other girls? Is he a flirt? Does he respect females in general?

3. How does he get along with adults? teachers? coaches? youth minister? Does he respect authority? Does he respect the law?

4. What kind of relationship does he have with his parents? Does he have problems at home? Does he blame his parents? How does his dad treat his mom? How does his mom treat his dad?

5. Does he say one thing and do another? Do you sometimes suspect he is lying? Have you ever caught him in a lie? Have you ever known him to be deceptive to other people?

6.  Is he selfish and self-centered, or does he think of others first?

7.  Does he respect God and have a growing relationship with Jesus Christ? If you are already dating him, is he the spiritual leader in your relationship? Does he initiate going to church or does he accompany you to church? Does he pray with you and for you? Is he on the same level as or higher spiritually than you?

8.  Does he drink alcohol or use drugs? Do you suspect that he has addictions to these or other things?

9.  What are his closest friends like? Do other people respect them?

10. Does he lose his temper easily, or is he sensible in working through problems in an appropriate way?

11. Have you known him long enough to see him in good times and bad times? How does he handle a crisis situation? Does he handle bad situations in a mature way?

12. How does he handle disagreements? If you already have a relationship with him, have you known him long enough to have a disagreement? Some disagreements are normal in a relationship. How you handle the process of working out the disagreement matters the most.

13. Does he ask you to do things you know are not right? Has he ever asked you to break the law or go against the rules? Does he pressure you to do things his way?

14. Has he ever been physically abusive to you or anyone else? Does he push you, hit you, or hurt you physically in any way?

The answers to these questions will tell you what kind of person he really is. If you spend mostly one-on-one time with him, you will not be able to see how he interacts with others. Going out in groups is a critical step in getting to know someone.

After you have the answers to the above questions, measure those answers against your dating standards. If he meets your standards, it is still crucial to guard your heart until your relationship has been tested for a long time. Focusing on friendship and not romance is a safe way to guard your heart.

Many girls make the tragic mistake of saying, "When we get married, he will be different. I will change him." Putting on a wedding ring is not magic. If a guy has bad character before he puts on the ring, he will still have bad character after he puts on the ring. If a guy doesn't respect females before he gets married, it will only be worse after he gets married. If he cheats with other girls before he gets married, he will cheat on his wife after he gets married. The ceremony and honeymoon do not transform bad character into good character. Some men do change later in life, but only because God changes them. A woman has never changed a man.

Statistics show that every fifteen seconds a woman is battered by her husband or boyfriend.[1] Nationally, 50 percent of all homeless women and children are on the streets because of violence in the home.[2] A child's exposure to the father's abusing the mother is the strongest risk factor for transmitting violent behavior from one generation to the next.[3]

If you see those small warning signs, don't ignore them. Your future and the future of your children and grandchildren depend on it! Many girls get into a romantic relationship with a guy and later realize he is abusive or has bad character. At that point, many guys will not give up. They will threaten, pursue, or even stalk a former girlfriend. Before you get into a romantic relationship and marry a guy, be sure he has good character and is not abusive.

The world tells a girl to follow her heart. Let's see what the Bible says about that. Read Jeremiah 17:9-10 and Proverbs 3:5-8. According to these verses, can you trust your heart? _____ Why?

_____

_____

Whom can you trust?

_____

_____

What will be the result of trusting the Lord?

_____

_____

_____

_____

_____

Getting to know someone takes a long time. Knowing if the guy you like is the one God has for you is a process. Let's see if we can summarize the process.

- Set your dating standards before beginning to date.
- If you see someone you are interested in, watch him in group settings for several months. Make sure you answer the character questions above.

- Be honest with yourself about his character flaws. Don't ignore the warning signs.
- Guard your heart by saving your kisses, saving your "I love you's," and avoiding tempting situations. *Don't follow your heart; follow God.* He will lead you to the right person. When he does, you will know it.
- Focus on friendship, not romance, until you have permission from God to make a commitment to that one certain guy.
- Keep your relationship with Jesus the center of your life.

You will never find a perfect guy because no one is perfect except Jesus Christ, but if a guy is out of control in any of the character areas discussed above, you might want to avoid dating him.

Read the following scriptures and see if you can determine the kind of guys with whom you should avoid building close relationships.

2 Corinthians 6:14________________________________

________________________________________________

❤ 1 Corinthians 15:33

________________________________________________

Proverbs 24:12____________________________________

When a Christian marries an unbeliever, many problems will arise in the future. Everything a Christian does should be centered on obedience to God. An unbeliever cannot understand this kind of life. When two people marry, they become one.

Have you ever thought about Siamese twins? What happens when one wants to go one way, and the other wants to go the opposite direction? There is frustration, arguing, and unhappiness. It's the same when a couple marries and they desire to live two different lifestyles. One or the other has to compromise and give up what he or she really desires. Can you guess which one usually gives in?

Often girls will deceive themselves by thinking they can win their lost boyfriend to the Lord. Out of twenty-five years in youth ministry, I have never seen this happen. The opposite has always proven to be true. First Corinthians 15:33 says, "Bad company corrupts good morals."

I have often heard the following: "If you eat with the pigs, you will smell like one."

"One bad apple ruins the whole basket."

"If you play with fire, you will get burned."

"Birds of a feather flock together."

Get the picture? These are old sayings you may never have heard. They have been passed down for generations and rightly so. They usually have proven to be true.

### Top Ten Guys to Avoid

Read over the list of character questions again listed on pages 90-91. Can you name the top ten characteristics you should avoid in the guys you date?

10. _____

9. _____

8. _____

7. _____

6. _____

5. _____

4. _____

3. _____

2. _____

1. _____

With the help of your parents or a godly mentor, write your dating standards. Before you begin, pray and ask God to show you the kind of young men you should date, what you should and should not do on dates, and what kind of goals you should set for yourself. In writing your standards, consider this: "The type of guy you should marry is found in places you should go."[4] Think about it. Put your standards up in your room where you will see them often. ☺

_____

_____

_____

_____

_____

_____

_____

_____

_____

_____

_____

## Deciphering Confusing Boy Behavior

Let's face it. Guys are hard to figure out. Sometimes guys will say and do things that totally confuse a girl. One girl set her dating standards high. All during high school, she focused on friendships and tried to guard her heart. She had one special friendship with a guy who exceeded all of her standards. On graduation night, he asked her to go out with him. During the summer their friendship grew. He made her feel like a princess. He did and said all the right things. He told her how much he loved her. He respected her in every way. He was preparing for ministry and was the most spiritually mature guy she had ever met. As time drew near for them to go away to college, they both felt sad. The colleges they had chosen were in different states. They spent as much time together as possible. The night before they had to leave for college, he wrote her a letter that any girl would cherish. The letter read:

My Dearest Britney,
I will miss you with all my heart when we have to leave each other. You are the light of my life. This summer has been the most wonderful time I have ever had. We both have to be strong. I will go to college and learn everything I can about being a godly man. You go to college and learn everything you can about being a godly woman. Then one day we will get married and have godly children.
I love you with all my heart,
Wes

Can you imagine how she must have felt? Any girl would consider that a marriage proposal! She left the next morning for college feeling on top of the world. She would miss Wes, but she had so much to learn to be ready for her life with him one day.

Wes called every day for the first week. Britney hurried back to her dorm room after classes so she would not miss his call. The first day he missed calling she passed it off, telling her friends he must be terribly busy. After a few weeks, the calls stopped completely. What could be wrong?

On his birthday, she called to wish him a happy birthday. She asked what he planned to do to celebrate. He nonchalantly answered, "Oh, I'm going to Susan's house. She's baking a birthday cake for me."

Britney could hardly choke back the tears. After a few seconds, she swallowed hard and asked, "Who is Susan?"

He replied, "Oh, just a girl I have been dating here at college."

Of course, Britney was devastated. When she burst into tears, he defended his actions. "You didn't expect me to sit here at college and not date anyone else, did you?"

During Christmas break, Wes called and asked Britney for a date New Year's Eve. She decided to confront him with the promises he made in the letter. He hardly even remembered writing the letter. He apologized for hurting her, and she never heard from him again.

Why did Wes write such a romantic letter if he didn't mean it? Was he a terrible person? Did he mean to hurt her? No, I don't think so. The truth is, he probably *did* mean what he said in the letter at the time, but he was not emotionally mature enough or ready to keep such a strong commitment. He did an unwise thing and made a promise he couldn't keep. Many times, a guy will say things just to make a girl feel good. Sometimes, he will not count the cost before making a statement or making a romantic gesture.

The bottom line is: Girls take comments and actions more seriously than guys intend them many times. Sometimes a guy will open the door for a girl and she will think he likes her, when the truth is, he is simply a polite guy. Continually guard your heart and do not deceive yourself. When Britney received the letter from Wes, she still should have guarded her heart. Can a girl do that on her own strength? No! She must depend on her security in Jesus Christ to meet her deepest heart needs.

The love relationship with your husband is an added special gift God has given you to make life more enjoyable and meaningful. God designed the husband-wife relationship to be a picture of our relationship with God. This relationship is meant to help us understand him better. When we step ahead of God's plan and make wrong choices in our love relationships, it alters our view of what our relationship with God should be.

In the beginning, God's plan for us was perfect. Unfortunately, sin has distorted God's plan for the family and that, in turn, distorts our view of God. If we will follow God's Word and be obedient to him, we can experience the joy and love he planned for us from the very beginning in a marriage relationship.

Not only do girls deceive themselves, guys deceive girls, girls deceive guys, but sometimes girlfriends deceive each other by encouraging their friend to read something into a relationship that is not really there. Be careful and don't be easily deceived or have a part in deceiving others.

When a guy says something that literally sends you into orbit, ask yourself, "Can he really deliver on that promise, or is it impossible for him at this time?" When a guy offers a kind gesture, accept it as a kind gesture. Don't blow his actions out of proportion. If Britney had been thinking with her brain instead of her heart, she would have realized that four years is a long time to sit and wait for someone in another state. They would only see each other at Christmas and for a few days in the summer. It was really unfair to expect them to sit in their dorm rooms and not enjoy college life. Britney kept her heart under lock and key the rest of her college days. God has blessed her with a wonderful husband who again exceeds her standards. Wes was a great guy, but God had another plan for Britney. Just because a guy meets your standards doesn't necessarily mean he is the one for you.

By setting standards, focusing on developing godly character, getting to know a guy before you give your heart to him, and thinking with your brain instead of your heart, you will be able to crack the code on guys. All these actions will protect you from the heartache of broken relationships and ruined lives. You will better be able to determine the right person with whom God intends for you to spend the rest of your life.

Write in the space below how God has spoken to you through this chapter. What steps do you plan to take in order to find God's best for you?

_____

_____

_____

_____

_____

## INSTANT MESSAGE

WannaBpretty2: I've got this terrible problem. My best friend is really gorgeous. All the girls at my school flip out when she talks to their boyfriends— yours truly included. I know she can't help being so beautiful. Why can't I be beautiful like her? My boyfriend says he doesn't like her, but I get really jealous when she flirts with him. My boyfriend is a really great, Christian guy, but I'm afraid he's going to be tempted by her. What should I do?

**VirtualYou77: Sounds like you are being hard on yourself. Let's try to see yourself through God's eyes and then you'll understand why your guy likes YOU instead of HER! We'll start with the inside and work our way to the outside. Sound okay?**

WannaBpretty2: Can't hurt. I guess I do need to look at myself differently. Can't seem to stop comparing myself to other people.

**VirtualYou77: Let's put on God's virtual glasses and look at reality.**

WannaBpretty2: Okay ... whatever that means....

**VirtualYou77: You'll understand soon. Trust me.**

# SIX

# The Reality of Virtue

What will they think of next?! Virtual reality is an awesome invention! You put on funny-looking glasses and it seems like you are involved in a real situation. The makeover God wants to do in your life from the inside out is a little bit like virtual reality. You put on God's glasses and look at yourself through his eyes. The only difference? His makeover is real, not an illusion.

Ron Hutchcraft has a Christian radio program called "A Word With You," and each day the transcript of his program is sent out to thousands of people through E-mail. One example he used perfectly describes what God can do in your life.

*Caterpillars are ugly. Now I don't mean to be critical, but let's face it, those hairy crawlers are not the beauty queens of the animal kingdom. I've never heard of anyone with a caterpillar collection, have you? Oh, I suppose someone could try a makeover on a caterpillar, you know, just shave off some of that hair, give him a little color ... but who could ever imagine that one of the uglier critters around could actually become one of the most beautiful creatures around—the butterfly! You don't see many pictures of caterpillars around, but you see pictures of butterflies everywhere! A critter covered with ugly black hair becomes a butterfly splashed with amazing colors. An animal that lives off the leaves of the ground becomes the connoisseur of flower nectar, ... and a creature that once crawled everywhere becomes one that can fly everywhere. We're not talking just a makeover here. We're talking miracle.*

God can perform the same kind of makeover miracle in your life as well. Let's look at this more....

Write the things you would like to change about yourself.☺

_____

_____

_____

_____

Now, from this list, write the things that are possible for you to change. For example, you may like to change your hairstyle or be more physically fit. It is possible to change that. On the other hand, you might like to be shorter. Cutting off your feet or head is about the only solution to that, and we all know that would only cause other problems! Seriously, there are some things you can change and others you cannot. Transfer your answers to the proper column in this chart and indicate whether you can change the characteristic or not.

| Inner Beauty Characteristic | Outer Beauty Characteristic | Can I Change it? YES | Can I Change it? NO |
|---|---|---|---|
|  |  |  |  |
|  |  |  |  |
|  |  |  |  |
|  |  |  |  |

Let's focus on the things we *can* change.☺

Maybe all of the things you would like to change are on the outside, but God wants to perform a miracle makeover in your life beginning on the inside. He wants to begin on the inside and transform you into a beautiful creature. He wants to get you off of a diet of leaves and onto a diet of flower nectar. He wants to get you off the ground and help you take to the air just like a butterfly.

Maybe you see yourself as a caterpillar. You are not satisfied with your body, hair, face, or anything else. You spend all your time trying to change your looks, improve yourself, or look and be like other people.

Many girls want to be accepted by their friends or get a boyfriend so desperately they will use makeup, clothes, or do things to their hair and body that are not flattering. Have you ever worn clothes or used make-up or had a hairstyle you didn't really like in order to be accepted or to get a boyfriend? Tell what you did.

_____

_____

_____

The world has convinced girls the only way to be beautiful and to get a guy is to show as much skin as possible, and dress as sexily and seductively as possible. Fashion magazines and movie stars set the standard for the way most girls dress and look. The malls are full of clothes and products to make you look sexy.

Let's face it. It's hard to find "clothes that don't expose." Commercials and advertisements focus on sex and dressing seductively. Why do you think this is true? ☺

_____

_____

_____

Any salesperson or businessperson will tell you that sex sells. Hollywood is not interested in you as a person. They are interested in one thing—making money. If you have a fashion magazine lying around, take a look at it. Write down as many things as you see in the magazine that focus on sex. Look at the advertisements, titles, models, and clothes and describe what you see. ☺

_____

_____

_____

_____

Read Proverbs 5:3, 6:24-25, and 7:21 and write the description of this woman. Describe how this woman with no character gets a man's attention. ☺

_____

_____

_____

Do fashion magazines, movies, and soap operas teach girls how to get their guys in the same way? Write down some headlines from the covers of some magazines near the checkout in the grocery store.

_____

_____

_____

Dress is a huge issue with teenage girls today. Back in Chapter Four, we discussed guys' perceptions of how girls dress. Remember, guys are turned on by three things: what they see, what they see, and what they see. Many girls make the comment, "I can dress any way I choose. If a guy gets turned on looking at me, that's *his* problem." Let's see what the Bible has to say about that. Read Proverbs 7:1-27. Focus on verse 10. What kind of dress do you think this verse describes? Think about the clothes you wear. Could any of your clothes be put into this category? Yes, young men are responsible for their actions. But women of all ages are also responsible for their actions.

According to Dr. Allen Jackson, professor of youth ministry at New Orleans Baptist Seminary, "There is a difference between dressing attractively and seductively. If a girl stops to truly examine herself in the mirror, she will know the difference, especially if she is a growing Christian."

Read Mark 9:42 and write the warning it gives in this verse.☺

_____

_____


Ouch! The Bible says it would be better to have a heavy stone around your neck and be thrown into the ocean than to cause a weaker person to stumble. That's pretty heavy. (No pun intended!) It seems like God takes that kind of thing pretty seriously. Girls who dress sensually, talk seductively, and tease guys sexually are at risk of causing guys to stumble.

Let's read what else Jesus had to say about this subject. Read Matthew 5:27-28 and write what it says. ☺

_____

_____

Jesus made some pretty strong comments about causing others to stumble by our example. We will talk about dress more in Chapter Eight.

King Solomon was a wise man. Proverbs 31 is a summary of the things his mother taught him about a virtuous woman. Read ❤ Proverbs 31:30 and write what you think it means in the space.

_____

_____

_____

_____

What does this verse mean when it says beauty is fleeting and charm is deceptive? ☺

_____

_____

_____

_____

As a girl grows older her body changes. Many women fear growing older. They will try anything to avoid gaining weight, getting wrinkles, getting gray hair, developing crow's-feet around their eyes and sagging body parts. But sooner or later, age creeps in and no matter what you do, your body changes. When that happens, will your husband still love you? Is your life over? Will you continue to dress and expose your body to keep your man? Will you still be attractive? It depends on what you do now. Let's think about this together.

Let's suppose you attract a guy with your body and your looks.

His focus is totally on how you look. The two of you get married and your body begins to change. Maybe you gain a little weight, get pregnant, or you don't have the money to purchase the kind of clothes you did before. He begins to make little comments about how you look. He makes a few suggestions and you try to please him, but because of circumstances beyond your control, you can't.

Later, you go to the doctor for a yearly checkup. Your greatest fear has come true. You have breast cancer. Will your husband still love you? Will he still want to be married to you? If he loves you only because of your looks, maybe not!

Let's consider another scenario. Suppose you attract a guy with sex. He thinks you are very good. Having sex with you makes him feel great and boosts his self-esteem. The two of you marry and you do everything to please him sexually. You try harder and harder, and he wants more and more. It seems really hard to satisfy him. One day, you find out you are pregnant. As time goes on, you begin to have problems with your pregnancy. The doctor tells you that sex will be dangerous to the baby, and until the baby is born, you cannot have sex. You go home and tell your husband. He blows up! "What? No sex for four months!" He begins to stay out later each night. Then one night he doesn't come home at all. Several days later, he comes in and tells you he has found someone else. When the sex wasn't there, the guy hit the road.

Are you beginning to get the picture? Whatever you do to catch your guy, you have to continue to keep him. The facts of life show that beauty will surely fade one day or could be taken away instantly in an accident or sickness. Sex is not possible 24/7 and sometimes not at all.

How can you be sure he loves you for who you are and not what you provide for him? Looks will change. Sex will change. You have no control over these things.

However, there is one thing you can control. In fact, it only grows better with time. That is your godly character. When your guy is attracted to your godly character first, he will be yours forever.

Let's see what God has to say about this. Read 1 Peter 3:3 and write what it says.

_____

_____

_____

Many women misunderstand this verse. They go to the extreme and say you should be homely and not dress attractively. The Bible does not teach this. Braiding your hair and wearing gold jewelry is not wrong in itself. God knows real beauty is not found on the outside. Outward beauty will fade, but inward beauty will only grow better.

Have you ever met someone for the first time and you thought that person was beautiful? Then, after you got to know them and saw their inner character, they didn't seem as beautiful? On the other hand, you met someone you thought was not attractive, but after you got to know the person, you thought he or she was beautiful? Most of us have. Which would you prefer to be?

Inner beauty affects outward beauty. God expects you to take care of your body and look your best. Chapter Eight focuses on outer beauty. But if you have bitterness and hatred built up inside, it affects your face and how you look. Have you ever met someone who always looked like they just swallowed a lemon? That person probably has hurt, bitterness, and bad character in her life. Read further in 1 Peter 3:4. Where should your beauty come from?

_____

_____

The first four words of Proverbs 31:30 say, "Do not be deceived...." Have you been deceived by the world into thinking that looks, sex, and your outward appearance are most important? If the answer is yes, write a prayer to God asking him to show you the truth.

_____

_____

Galatians 5:19-21 describes the characteristics that cause us to be like the ugly caterpillar. Write each characteristic and a brief meaning. If you don't know the meaning, look in the concordance of your Bible or in a dictionary. This is a little more work, but it is important to know characteristics that should be avoided in life.☺

| Characteristic | Definition |
|---|---|
|  |  |
|  |  |
|  |  |
|  |  |
|  |  |

If you desire to be a young woman of character and beauty, can you have these characteristics in your life?

Which of these things do you need to get rid of in your life?

_____

_____

First John 1:9 says, "If we confess our sins, he is faithful to forgive us our sins and to cleanse us from all unrighteousness." Stop now and write a prayer asking God's forgiveness for these things. Confess the sin that has developed this bad characteristic in your life.

_____

_____

_____

Inward beauty, character, and virtue are developed over time as you allow God to work in your life. As you develop your relationship with Jesus, and learn more about him and what he wants for your life, your character and virtue will blossom. Only God can perform this miracle makeover in your life.

In God's Word, Galatians 5:22-23 lists the characteristics the Holy Spirit wants to produce in your life. Name them. ☺

_____

_____

_____

As these characteristics develop, you will grow from a caterpillar into a cocoon and finally a beautiful butterfly. The caterpillar goes through a process to become a butterfly. It doesn't happen overnight.

First, the caterpillar spins a cocoon. That's pretty hard work! Then after a period of time, the caterpillar struggles and stretches and works out of the cocoon to become a creature of beauty.

A little girl once found a cocoon. She brought it into the house and her mother explained that one day, if she was patient, a beautiful butterfly would come out of the cocoon. The little girl waited anxiously. One day, she could wait no longer. She took her little scissors and cut the cocoon open and helped the butterfly out. It crawled pitifully along the kitchen cabinet. The little girl began to cry, and her mother came in to see what was wrong. She wanted so desperately for the beautiful butterfly to flutter away. Her mother explained that the butterfly would never be able to fly. You see, the struggle to get out of the cocoon strengthens the wings and enables the butterfly to soar.

As you grow into a teenager and young woman, you will experience numerous struggles. You will face problems with friends, guys, self-esteem, and choices. If you are patient and follow God's plan for your life each day, God will perform that miracle makeover you long for. Each step along the way is an incredible process. It's not the finished product but the process that is beautiful. You will be a creature of beauty and significance as you grow and follow God's plan for your life. You will soar to heights you never dreamed you would go. You will be beautiful from the inside out. Not only will your friends look up to you, but also you will be irresistible to godly guys. Your inward character and the beauty that comes from that will give you the virtual makeover. Your character and virtue can never be taken away; they will only get better with time. This is the reality of virtue.

## INSTANT MESSAGE

Nlovew2guys: I'm in big trouble. I'm in love with two guys at the same time! I have been going out with a guy for three months. I really love him and I think he loves me. At least he tells me all the time. Then I met this other guy last weekend. We really hit it off, if you know what I mean. Instant attraction. Now I think I'm in love with this guy, too! I have feelings for both guys, and I don't want to give up either one. They don't know about each other, and I'm a nervous wreck trying to keep them apart. What should I do?

**VirtualYou77: Sounds like you need a break to think this thing through. Sometimes it's hard to tell the difference between infatuation and true love. Let's try to define love and then go from there.**

Nlovew2guys: I'm willing to try anything. Can't eat. Can't sleep. I'm worried about this whole mess.

**VirtualYou77: Okay, let's get busy and you'll have this thing figured out in no time.**

Nlovew2guys: Thanks! I knew you would come through.

# SEVEN

# Search Engine for True Love

When surfing the Net for information, it's important to know which search engine to use. Using the wrong search engine may prevent you from finding all the information you need. It's basically the same with love. The old saying "looking for love in all the wrong places" hits home with many girls today. As we saw in Chapter Five, finding true love requires a long process. Let's think about some of the steps in finding true love.

First, write your definition of love. ☺

_____

_____

_____

_____

## Learning to Love

An infant begins learning how to love and be loved from the time of birth. A person goes through several stages in life learning how to love at different levels. There are seven stages: infant, toddler, child, preteen, teen, young adult, and adult. By the time a person reaches the adult stage, he or she should know how to love and be loved. At that time, a person should be ready for a husband-wife relationship and a parent-child relationship. If one of the stages is skipped, the skills to adequately love and receive love are lacking.

When a child grows up with good role models, the process is easier and more complete. One signal of entry into young adulthood is the ability to appropriately deal with intimacy.

Many girls try to skip the steps of learning and go straight into a love relationship with a guy. Many couples experience problems in their marriages and relationships with their children because they have been denied or have skipped the important steps of learning how to love. Let's look at these stages of learning.

1. *Infant.* As an infant, you experienced love by having your needs met, that is, having your diapers changed and being fed, bathed, and kept warm. You experienced touch when your mother held and rocked you. At that point, you began bonding with your parents and siblings. You were able to recognize familiar faces and understand language. What is your first memory of being held or loved?

_____

_____

_____

2. *Toddler.* As a toddler you learned to share (the hard way sometimes!). You continued to experience bonding with parents and express feelings in words. You continued learning how to receive love by having your needs met, being held, rocked, and cared for. Imitating actions of love by repeating, "I love you," and throwing kisses are all a part of being a toddler. During this time you continued learning to understand language and express needs, wants, fears, and desires through language. At this point, you learned there were consequences for bad actions. Can you briefly write a story

your parents have told about you when you were this age?

_____

_____

_____


3. *Child.* As a child, you continued learning to share. You began expressing feelings in complete sentences. Instead of imitating love, you began showing love spontaneously. You learned you could help others. You learned to line up and take turns. You learned manners and showing respect and the consequences when you didn't. Hopefully, at this point your parents let you make age-appropriate decisions. Tell about a time when you suffered consequences because of your actions.

_____

_____

_____


4. *Preteen.* Oh, boy! Your preteen years were when you learned that boys really don't have cooties. You noticed the opposite sex and learned age-appropriate social skills. You started growing out of childish ways. All the while you were continually learning more about respect, and showing and receiving love. You began expressing feelings verbally and listening to the feelings of others on a deeper level. Can you think of the first boy you "liked"? How did you handle the relationship? (Don't laugh too hard!)

_____

_____

_____

Would you handle a relationship the same way today? If not, how would you handle it differently?

_____

_____

_____

5. *Teen.* As a teen, you have begun to interact on a deeper level with the opposite sex. You are maturing in social skills and beginning to desire independence. You are setting standards and goals for your life. Distinguishing between good and bad character is a vital learning experience as a teenager. You are still learning to respect, and how to show and receive love. From now on your decision-making is a vital part of learning to love. You are learning to become more responsible, express feelings, and listen to the feelings of others. Learning that "the world does not revolve only around me" usually happens in the teen years also. Name one way you have matured since you were a preteen. If you are not there yet, name one way you would like to mature in the next year.

_____

_____

_____

6. *Young Adult.* When you graduate from high school and go away to college, you become more independent from your parents. You are forced to make decisions independently. You learn by making mistakes and then, hopefully, not making those same mistakes again. You learn how to become more responsible financially. In college, you experience living with a roommate, which helps you

continue to learn respect and how to show love. You learn that it's "not just about me" at a deeper level. What goals would you like to accomplish in your life at this stage?

_____

_____

_____

As you can see, if any of the natural steps of learning how to love and be loved are skipped, important relationship skills are missed. When a girl focuses on friendships, guards her heart, and goes through the natural steps of learning how to love and be loved, then she will be ready for a husband-wife love relationship as well as other relationships.

Isn't God awesome! He knows the best way for you. ❤ Read Jeremiah 29:11. Write this verse using your name where it says "you."

_____

_____

_____

### Defining Love

Many people have tried to come up with a good definition of love, but it's really hard. Let's see exactly what God's definition of love is. Read 1 Corinthians 13:4-8 and list the ingredients of love. ☺

_____

_____

_____

Look at your definition at the beginning of this chapter and compare it to God's ingredients. Many people try to describe love as a feeling, but God describes love as an action. Love is patient. Love is kind.

I remember once a person did and said some really terrible things about my family and me. I felt deeply hurt. This person was a member of my church and worked with the youth. I had to see the person every Sunday and Wednesday. The comments continued and I tried to forgive this person, but needless to say I didn't have good feelings in my heart. I tried to pray but I didn't feel love in my heart. I felt guilty, because I knew God wanted me to love others. I didn't have problems loving other people but this one person was my "heavenly sandpaper." God was trying to smooth off my rough edges by allowing me to experience this persecution.

I was desperate. I called a godly woman I respected, who had been a mentor to me for many years. I knew she would help me. Sometimes I didn't want to hear what she said because it was not comfortable, but I knew she would lead me in the right direction. She told me something I will never forget. It has helped me deal with many difficult people since that time. She said, "Jimmie, God doesn't require you to like this person. He only requires you to love this person. You may not have loving feelings in your heart, but love is an action." She told me to read 1 Corinthians 13:4-8 and practice what it said.

I went back to church and I was patient. I was kind. I overcame my feelings of jealousy toward this person. I didn't rejoice when this person got what was coming. My feelings began to change over time. This person's actions began to change in response to my actions. We were not best friends and didn't hang out together, but we did respect each other from that time on.

Learning to love and respect others is a necessary foundation for a marriage love relationship. Is there someone you do not like but need to love? Write a code here that will remind you who the person is._____

Name the steps you will take this week to love this person.

_____

_____

_____

### Getting Rid of Childish Ways

The entire chapter of 1 Corinthians 13 is known as "the love chapter." There is one verse, however, that doesn't seem to fit. It's well worth your time to figure out what this verse means if you want to experience ultimate love in your relationships. Read ♥ 1 Corinthians 13:11 and write what it says.

_____

_____

Let's think about this more. Name some childish ways. Hang with me, because this is important. What do little kids do when they don't get their way? ☺

_____

_____

_____

If you have younger brothers or sisters or have been around children at all, you know that children are very self-centered. When they do not get their way, they will pout, cry, throw temper tantrums, tattletale, throw things, hit, scream, yell, kick, bite, run away and hide, manipulate, beg, take their toys and go home, try to make you feel sorry for them, be bossy, hold their breath to scare you, and do anything else they think will work. Hopefully, as the child grows bigger and matures, these childish ways diminish.

Think about your life and how you deal with other people. Do you show childish ways in your relationships with other people? Do you pout to get your way? Do you cry crocodile tears to make someone feel sorry for you? Do you lose your temper and yell at others? Do you call your friends and say, "Do you know what 'so and so' did to me?" This is the adult form of being a tattletale. Do you throw things when you get mad? Are you ever physically aggressive when you are trying to get your way? Do you ever walk out, slam the door, get in your car and speed away, or go in your room and turn on the CD player instead of dealing with a situation in a mature way? Many times childish ways are carried into adulthood.

Sometimes, because significant adults in our lives model these kinds of behaviors in front of us as children and teenagers, we think it's normal behavior. We learn these childish ways and accept them as a normal lifestyle. The extremely sad part comes when we have children. We model those behaviors and pass them down to our children and grandchildren. This destructive cycle is called generational sin. Sins can be passed down for many generations in families. It only takes one person to put away childish ways and begin to live a godly lifestyle to stop this type of generational sin. The Bible is very specific about putting away childish ways as we grow older and more mature.

Why do you think this verse about childish ways is in the love chapter? Could it have something to do with love? Write your thoughts.

_____

_____

_____

_____

_____

_____

_____

In God's wisdom, he knows childish ways will destroy love relationships. Childish ways will destroy a parent-child relationship. Childish ways will destroy a husband-wife relationship. Childish ways will destroy a friend-to-friend relationship. Childish ways will destroy a church, a family, a business, or a youth group.

Each time you pout, cry, or yell to get your way, it drives a little wedge between you and the other person. True love thinks about what is best for the other person, not what is best for self.

Most importantly, childish ways hinder your relationship with God. When a person thinks selfishly all the time, it is hard to think about God and focus on him. The sins of childish ways block intimacy with him. God cannot be joined with sin. Childish ways, if left alone to grow and ripen, will sooner or later destroy the most important love relationship you will ever have—your relationship with God, who loves you more than anyone.

Many times, it's hard to see childish ways because they are so much a part of how we act. Write down all the childish ways you can think of in your life at this point.

_____

_____

_____

_____

When I first learned this principle of God's Word, I worked hard every day to get rid of childish ways. I worked on getting rid of one childish way at a time so I would not feel overwhelmed. I prayed every day for God to show me childish ways in my life and help me to overcome the temptation to act childishly. I matured both emotionally and spiritually that year.

I thought I was doing pretty well and had conquered those childish ways in my life. About a year later, a co-worker said something to embarrass me. I immediately walked away and went upstairs in the church. Another minister was standing there, and I said, "Do you know what 'so and so' just said to me?"

Immediately it was like God said, "Tattletale, Tattletale!" I stopped dead in my tracks.

The other minister replied, "No, what?" I stared at him for a minute and said, "Oh, nothing, it wasn't important." God had shown me a childish way in my life even a year later. No matter how hard I try, sometimes those ugly childish ways pop up. But they are much easier to recognize now, and I stop and pray that God will help me and forgive me each time I act childishly.

Ask God to show you one childish way he wants you to work on in your life this week. Write it down and pray that God will help you overcome this bad habit in your life.

_____

_____

_____

_____

_____

_____

## Infatuation vs. Commitment

When I was a teenager, older folks called it "puppy love." I always wondered what "old dogs" felt like when they were in love. Well, it's not much different. The truth is you can have those feelings of attraction at any time in your life, for many different people. God has given humans the wonderful ability to feel attracted to the opposite sex. When you become engaged or get married, that ability doesn't shut down like a computer when it's turned off. You still have the ability to be attracted. Many women mistake that attraction for true love. Let's think about it....

A girl I once knew called me for advice. I'll call her Tiffany. She was terribly upset and didn't know what to do. She had dated a guy for several years. Now they were engaged. He was a wonderful guy, met all her standards, and cared deeply for her. The date was set. The wedding dress was bought. Then she met a guy at work to whom she was very attracted. He said and did all the right things. They began to meet for dinner and talked for hours each time. He knew she was engaged, but continued to pursue her.

Tiffany was very confused. She had made a commitment to her fiancé but she wasn't sure she loved him anymore. Her feelings for the new guy seemed to be growing every day. Her heart fluttered when she heard his voice on the phone. She couldn't eat. She couldn't sleep. He was all she thought about.

After talking through the situation, I reminded her that true love is not a feeling; it is a commitment. Feelings come and go. You will not wake up every day and feel loving toward your husband. Some days it will be hard. Some days you will feel like giving up. I reminded her not to depend entirely on her feelings, to think through the situation with her mind and not her emotions, and to pray and ask God to show her which man she should marry.

In the end, she decided to break her engagement and cancel the wedding. Notes were mailed to the guests, informing them the wedding was cancelled. Her fiancé was brokenhearted. Her family and friends were shocked.

She informed the man whom she felt so much love for that she was no longer engaged and they could now be together forever. A terrible look of fright appeared on his face. He began to make excuses not to be with her and soon she found that he was seeing another girl who was also committed to someone. It was easy for him to pursue a girl who was engaged or dating someone else. This kind of relationship required no commitment from him.

Tiffany began to realize that people don't really *fall* in love; they *commit* to love. If you *fall in love* it will be easy to *fall out of love*. If you commit to love, it will last a lifetime if you stay true to that commitment. There is a happy ending to this story. Her fiancé was still committed to her even though she broke the engagement. She began to see what an awesome guy she had in the first place. A few months later they had a wonderful wedding and have committed to love each other for a lifetime. This was a lesson well learned that will save her much heartache in the future.

Just for future reference, what should you do if you meet someone, feel attracted, develop the relationship, get God's permission, commit to love, get married, and then meet another man to whom you are physically attracted?

_____

_____

_____

_____

You got it! The smartest things you can do are walk away from the other guy and do not go to that second step of developing a relationship.

Keep in your mind that love is not a feeling, it is an action, and true love is a commitment for a lifetime that is not to be taken lightly.

Begin to pray that God will show you that special someone in your life WHEN you are ready. Ask God to help you go through the process of learning to love, defining love, and putting away childish ways. When you are totally dependent on him for your security and you love him with your whole heart, then and only then will you be ready for a lifetime love relationship and commitment with a man. Write your thoughts to God.

_____

_____

_____

## INSTANT MESSAGE

WannaNulook: I'm totally confused about make-up, clothes, and how I look. Last month I spent my whole allowance buying make-up and clothes I saw in a magazine. It looked great in the magazine but terrible on me. The make-up was all wrong. Some guys laughed at my clothes and, to top it off, I'm broke. I thought I could save money so I tried to cut my own hair. Disaster!! I wish I could just have a new body that would look like the models in that magazine. I hate the way I look!!

**VirtualYou77: Simmer down, girlfriend! We all feel that way sometimes. Don't give up. We can work through this together. There are a few basic things you need to learn, and then it will all come together. I'm sure you have lots of potential, and we can find it if you access your positives!**

WannaNulook: Thanks. I knew I could count on you. I really didn't mean what I said about hating the way I look. I'm just frustrated.

**VirtualYou77: That's okay. Let's get started learning those basics. Are you ready?**

WannaNulook: You bet!

# EIGHT

# Access Your Positives!

Your computer has thousands of features on it available for you to use. For most people the problem is knowing how to access these features. It is the same with you! God has given you wonderful physical features, and it's important to learn how to access them to look your best.

Let's face it! Girls love tips for make-up, hairstyles, nails, the latest fashions, losing weight, and skin care. I don't think there is a teenage girl alive who doesn't want to look her very best. If you pick up the latest fashion magazines, you will find hundreds of products, clothes, and gimmicks to make you beautiful. The only problem is you can spend your whole allowance and still not find the look you want.

How do you know which shampoo to buy to get flowing, silky, super-straight strands? Or would you look best with a bob cut accented with chunky layers? Which make-up should you buy to make your skin flawless and smooth? What if you look like a clown after applying your blush? How do you know which clothes will enhance your body shape and take pounds off in the right places? Which diet works best? There's low fat, low carbohydrates, vegetarian, high protein, all liquids, no sugar, and on and on we could go. All of these questions are legitimate. You will find a hundred answers to each of these questions in fashion magazines. How do you know which one is right?

We have already learned that true beauty comes from the inside, but God wants us to take care of our bodies and look our best on the outside as well. Many girls are not satisfied with the way they look and are constantly on the search for a new hairdo, the latest fashions in clothes, or a new twist in make-up that will make them drop-dead gorgeous. How do you find the answers to these questions?

The answers are out there. You just have to know where to find them. Every day I find features on my computer that help me access information. You have positive features also! Now we have to figure out how to access them!

## A Good Foundation

Don't freak out! There are absolute truths that will help you see yourself from God's perspective and give you a good foundation. An absolute truth is true in the past, in the present, and in the future, for every person who has ever lived, is living now, and will ever live in the future. Absolute truths are found in the Bible.

There are also a few basic principles that will help you look your very best. Principles are basic rules that work in general. First, let's think about three absolute truths.

*Truth #1:* **God made you exactly the way he wants you to look.** He knows everything about you. He knew if curly hair would look best with your face shape or if straight hair would do the job. He knew what color hair would look best with your skin color. God planned how you would look before he made you inside your mother's womb. He knew what size nose and ears to put on your head. He knew how tall he wanted you to be and why he wanted you to look the way you do.

Read Matthew 10:29-31. What do these verses tell you about how God feels about you? ☺

_____

_____

_____

_____

Read Psalm 139:13-14. What do these verses tell you about God's part in your creation? ☺

_____

_____

_____

Do you see yourself as fearfully and wonderfully made? How do you think God feels when you criticize the creation he has custom-designed? There is no other person on this earth exactly like you. God sees you as beautiful, and he made you for a purpose.

Maybe you were born with a disability. So was Moses! He had a speech impediment. Let's see what God told him. Read Exodus 4:10-11 and write what God said.

_____

_____

_____

_____

Wow! That's incredible! But maybe you have been injured in an accident or injured in another way. God is still in control. God did not cause the injury, but he allowed it to happen. He will use something bad in a wonderful way. He has a plan for your life!

I once met a person who was injured by a drunk driver. This person will be totally deaf for a lifetime. I have seen God use this situation to reach the lives of many people. Like Moses, the girl with disabilities must allow God to work his plan through her.

There are numerous things you can do to improve your looks that are okay with God, but your basic design is a beautiful creation he designed for himself and his purpose. Do you know that you fit into God's overall kingdom plan? He knew exactly what you would look like, what your IQ would be, and how he wants to use you. Refer to your memory verse from Chapter Seven and write it here.

_____

_____

_____

_____

God made you. He has a plan for you. He knew exactly how you needed to look to accomplish his plan. He wants you to be successful and have a wonderful future. Most of all, he wants to give you hope. Write a prayer to God telling him how you feel right now.

_____

_____

_____

_____

_____

*Truth # 2:* **Your body is the temple of the Holy Spirit, and you are not your own.** Read 1 Corinthians 6:19-20. What do you think verse 20 means when it says you were bought with a price? ☺

_____

_____

To whom does this verse say your body and spirit belong? ☺

_____

_____

Think about what it means to glorify God with your body. Name ways you can glorify God in the following areas: ☺

1. The way you talk about your body

_____

_____

2. The way you dress

_____

_____

3. The way you use your body

_____

_____

4. The things you put into your body

_____

_____

Name ways girls abuse their bodies and choose not to glorify God with their bodies. ☺

_____

_____

_____

Write a prayer to God asking him to help you change one bad habit you have regarding your body. Be specific.

_____

_____

_____

_____

***Truth #3:* God wants you to have self-control over your body and how you look.** Galatians 5:22 says that self-control is a fruit of the Spirit. That means when you accept Christ and the Holy Spirit comes to live in your heart and life, you will have access to the unlimited power of God. God's power plus your own discipline will result in self-control. God wants you to live a well-balanced life. He wants you to set priorities according to his Word so you can become exactly what he planned. Are there areas related to your body and how you look that are out of control? Do you let others dictate how you dress, eat, exercise, and treat your body? Write your thoughts and ask God to show you these areas.

_____

_____

_____

_____

It is important to avoid developing addictive behaviors. Many addictions develop in the teen years and continue into adult life, becoming worse with time. Addictions are more than bad habits. Addictions, if left alone, can control every area of your life.

Addictions begin in your mind. You begin to think about a feeling, substance, person, or act you think would satisfy the longing inside you. Then you begin to do whatever it takes to get it. You think you cannot live without this person, thing, or feeling. People can become addicted to all kinds of things—alcohol, drugs, shopping, food, sexual feelings, relationships, and being in control. When you are addicted to something, you feel relief for a short time when you get it. Soon the relief wears off and you begin to feel the need for it again.

Chemical addictions are dangerous to your health and life. Addictions to alcohol, drugs, tobacco, and inhalants can be deadly for teenagers. Many teens die from acute alcohol poisoning each year. Drug overdose, lung and heart disease from smoking, and irreversible brain and liver damage from inhalants are all potential outcomes of addictions for teens. Eating disorders also fall into the category of addictions. Bulimia, anorexia, overeating, or excessive dieting can also damage your body and health, sometimes resulting in death. Anorexia and bulimia can affect the health of your teeth, your reproductive organs, your skin, and other organs in your body.

If you or one of your friends think you have an addiction to any of these substances, or an eating disorder, it is important to talk with an adult you trust. Addictions will not go away without treatment. They will only become worse. Medical help and psychological counseling are needed to overcome most addictions. God wants you to be in control of your body. He doesn't want you to be controlled by addictions.

Addictions also affect how you look. Drinking alcohol excessively, smoking cigarettes, or using drugs will damage your health and affect your looks. You will look old and wrinkled before your time. According to *The American Dietetic Association's Complete Food and Nutrition Guide*, drinking large amounts of alcohol is linked to health problems such as high blood pressure, stroke, heart disease, certain cancers, birth defects, and diseases of the liver and pancreas.[1] Alcohol is high in calories and provides no nutrition. No amount of make-up or beauty products can hide the effects of bad health caused from substance abuse.

Name the three absolute truths discussed in this chapter.

1. _____

2. _____

3. _____

God wants you to accept your body the way he chose to make you. He wants you to glorify him with your body. He wants you to be in control of your body. These are foundational truths you can count on.

## Accessories Liven Up the Foundation

Now that we have learned to accept our bodies the way God made them, what can we do to make the most of what we have? Make-up, clothes, manicures, exercise, and nutrition are all accessories that put the finishing touches on the foundation God has given us.

Here are some basic principles regarding those accessories:

***Principle #1:*** **Develop a lifestyle of eating healthy, well-balanced meals**. This will not only keep your body healthy but will help you maintain the appropriate weight for your body size. Eating too many sweets, binge dieting, and greasy foods from fast-food restaurants will prevent you from looking your best. Greasy foods will affect your hair, skin, and weight. Most fast-food restaurants encourage you to "super size" your order. This is a no-no because it exceeds the amount of food any person should eat at one sitting.

A good example of the kinds of food and how much you should eat is on the back of most bread packages. It's called the food pyramid. The food pyramid shows you how to balance your food amounts from each food group so you will have the right nutrients and calories your body needs. The food pyramid also shows you which foods to limit, like fats and sugars. Each food group provides specific nutrients your body needs. For example, milk provides the calcium needed for good healthy bones. Many times we care about our clothes, our make-up, and our shoes. All of those things can be replaced, but our bones can't. We only have one body, and it cannot be replaced. What can you begin doing differently to keep your body healthy? ☺

_____

_____

_____

Go get the bread bag! It can be a good friend in helping you know the right kinds of food to eat to have a beautiful body.

*Principle #2:* **Drink plenty of water each day.** Your body needs water to get rid of wastes. It carries nutrients to your cells and helps to regulate your body temperature. Most doctors say at least eight cups of water are needed each day to keep your body healthy.

Some teens drink only soft drinks and very little water. Soft drinks are loaded with sugar and supply few nutrients for the body. Most soft drinks have caffeine, which acts as a mild diuretic, increasing water loss through urination. So, when drinking soft drinks, you are actually adding unnecessary calories and losing liquids instead of adding liquids to your body. Milk and fruit juices (without added sugar) are also healthy liquids to drink. Drinking water can actually help you lose those added pounds!

*Principle #3:* **Ask your doctor about taking a multi-vitamin, especially if you don't get a well-balanced diet.** Many teens skip meals and eat from fast-food restaurants often. A daily vitamin will take up the slack when you forget to eat your veggies and drink your milk. Keep a list of foods you eat and liquids you drink for a week. Evaluate the list to see if you are eating healthy foods and drinking enough liquids to keep your body in good shape. Make sure you don't overdose on vitamins. This can be harmful as well.

*Principle #4:* **Get the right amount of exercise.** Teens are watching more TV and sitting in front of computers more today than ever before. Schools have cut many physical education programs due to lack of funding.

Physical activity is important to help you look your best, feel your best, and do your best. How can you get enough exercise to keep your body healthy? If your school offers physical education or intra-mural sports, get involved. If you are not the athletic type, there are other activities you can do to get the right amount of exercise.

Take a walk around the neighborhood several times a week with a friend or family member. Take a prayer walk every day. This means you walk and pray at the same time. This would cover your physical and spiritual exercise! Exercise with an aerobics or Jazzercise video. Invite a friend to join you. Join a health club. Ride a bicycle. Jump rope. Swim. Take the stairs. Do anything except sit on your "tush" and watch the tube! Seriously, watching TV and sitting in front of your computer will add those unwanted pounds and cause you to feel tired and run down. Be active and make sure you have fun doing it!

***Principle #5:* When considering make-up, ask a professional for advice.** Most department stores and make-up companies have trained professionals who can tell you what colors look good, what the latest styles in make-up are, and what beauty products work well with your skin type. Most of the time this kind of advice is free. A skilled professional make-up artist can show you how to apply make-up in a way that will enhance your natural beauty and prevent you from looking like Bozo the clown. The principle "less is more" usually works well when applying make-up.

Many teens develop acne at some point. The best way to have healthy skin is to eat a well-balanced, nutritious diet, keep your skin clean, and get enough rest. If acne develops, it may be related to hormonal changes that occur during the teen years. If acne becomes persistent or severe, see your doctor. Over-the-counter medications may work for mild acne, but in some cases can make it worse. Your doctor will determine the cause and know which medication will work best for your skin type.

***Principle #6:*** **When considering hairstyles and products for your hair, your best resource is a good hair stylist**. A trained professional will be able to tell you what the latest hairstyles are, which ones will look good for your hair type and facial features, and which products will be best for your hair. You may have to shop around to find a person you really like and trust.

When coloring, perming, or cutting your hair, it is usually best to let a professional do the job. Mixing certain dyes and perming solutions together or leaving chemicals on your hair too long can damage your scalp and hair, or even make your hair fall out.

One girl decided to highlight her own hair with the help of a girlfriend. They bought the kit and when they got home, the cap was missing. She decided to go ahead and try to put the solution on her hair without pulling it through the cap. She ended up looking like a skunk with an orange stripe. Oh, boy! Many tears were shed over that situation. If you make a wrong choice like this, the only solution at this point is a cute hat! Using a professional hair stylist may cost a little more, but it will be worth it in the end.

***Principle #7:*** **Get the right amount of sleep and rest.** Most doctors say teens need at least eight hours of sleep each night. Most teens don't get it. With homework, school activities, church activities, family time, and all the other activities going on in your life, it is hard to get in bed in time to get enough sleep. A fifteen-minute nap in the afternoon will help you feel rested and give the boost you need to make it through the rest of the day.

*Principle #8:* **Choose and wear clothes that flatter your body and make you look attractive versus clothes that make you look sexy and sensual.** When choosing clothes, ask yourself these questions:

- Am I choosing these clothes because I like them and they look good on me, or am I choosing them because they are the latest fad?
- Is this piece of clothing a good use of my money? Will it last? Will it still be in style next month?
- Does this piece of clothing fit well?
- Do my clothes show my body and make me look sexy?
- Will this piece of clothing tempt guys to look at me with lust?
- Is this the image I want to portray with my body?
- Do my clothes help my body to glorify God?

Let's face it. It's hard to find clothes that don't show off your body and give you a sexy, sensuous look. Styles and the latest fads promote sex. Why? Sex sells. Does this mean you have to dress like an old woman, or look old-fashioned? No! Don't give up. There are stylish clothes that look good and don't make you look like you are ready for a night on the street corner.

What do guys think about the latest, sexy, sensual fashions? In asking guys of different ages this question, I have found some pretty interesting answers. Remember what we learned in Chapter Four. Guys are turned on by three things: what they see, what they see, and what they see. Some guys like sexy clothes, because it gives them a turn-on. It actually has nothing to do with the girl; it's the look they like. Some guys are embarrassed and feel guilty when they lust, because they are striving to be godly young men. Some guys ignore it, because they are immune. When you see something over and over again, soon it's nothing new and exciting. Some guys are grossed out and disgusted that girls don't have more self-respect. Let's turn the scenario around and see if we can put the shoe on the other foot for a change.

What would you think about a guy who always wore muscle shirts to show off his body? He wears muscle shirts to school, to church, on dates, to nice restaurants. He wears them everywhere! (No matter what he looks like!) He might be skinny with no muscles. He might be overweight with stretch marks. He might have a good body, with huge muscles that shine like he is on stage in a bodybuilding contest. Get a good mental picture in your mind. Be truthful. What would you think about him? ☺

_____

_____

Okay, next scenario. What would you think about a guy who wears those tight little brief-style bathing suits all the time to show his stuff? (Again, no matter what he looks like!) He wears them to school, to church, on dates, to nice restaurants. He may be skinny, overweight, or good-looking. What would you think about him? Be honest! ☺

_____

_____

Your first thought may be, "That's not the style." But what if it were? Would you be grossed out? Would you think the guy was vain and thought he looked good, even if he didn't? Would you think he was sexy? Would you lust after him? Would that cause you to stumble? Would you be tempted or turned off? Would you think he is ridiculous? These are all legitimate questions that only you can answer.

Most godly guys want a girl who respects herself and her body. A godly guy doesn't want other guys looking at his girl with lust. We have already talked about dressing in a way that causes a guy to stumble. Think about your clothes, the way you dress, and ask God if there are things you need to change in order to glorify him. Write his answer here. ☺

_____

_____

_____

*Principle #9:* **Think carefully before you go with a new fad.** Ask yourself these questions before getting involved with a new fad.

- Am I doing something permanent to my body that I may regret later in life? When this fad goes out, will I be stuck with it?
- Am I doing this because it makes me look better or am I doing it to be accepted by my friends?
- Do my parents approve of this fad? If not, why? Do they have a good reason?
- Is it possible this fad may harm my body in any way?
- Does this fad glorify God?

A good example of a popular fad that may cause harm to your body is covered in a question asked on the Center for Disease Control website:

Q) Can I get HIV from getting a tattoo or through body piercing?

A) A risk of HIV transmission (among other diseases) does exist if instruments containing blood are not sterilized or disinfected properly.

The last question is the most important. Does this fad glorify God? Some people use the excuse that God looks at the heart and not the outward appearance to justify dressing any way they want and doing things to their bodies. In 1 Samuel 16:7 we find it to be true that God looks at the heart. How do you think your heart condition will affect the way you dress and what you do to your body? ☺

_____

_____

_____

When a girl's heart is right with God, and she is secure in her relationship with him, she will want to glorify God with her body, her dress, her actions, and her whole being. What is your heart condition today? Write a letter to God about your heart and how you feel inside.

_____

_____

_____

Every girl wants to look her best. A makeover causes you to feel fresh and exciting. Becoming beautiful on the outside will not make you beautiful on the inside. However, allowing God to change your heart along with a few basic foundational truths and some basic principles to guide your choices for your appearance, you can have a miracle makeover that will guide you in becoming everything God intended you to be when he created you.

It's fun to experiment with new clothes and try new hairstyles, different make-up, and other products. Don't throw out the fun things, but make sure you line up with God's purpose for your looks and your health in everything you do.

Look for *Virtual You!* conferences on our websites! You will have a great time attending interactive workshops that give you tips on make-up, hairstyles, clothing styles, exercise, nutrition, and large group sessions that deal with deep heart issues! Check out these sites: www.girlsministry.org and www.girlsenrichmentministry.org.

## Conclusion

# From Girls to Women With Few Regrets

I'd like to conclude this book with an important question: "When you grow to be an old woman, will you look back on your life and have many regrets?"

Maybe your first thought is, "I can't answer that, I'm only a teenager!" Truthfully, now is the perfect time to answer it. If you decide now that the answer will be, "No, I will not look back and have many regrets," and you base your decisions in life on God's Word, then you will have less regret to deal with when you get old.

In summarizing this book, we need to look at the building blocks that will help you become what God wants you to become in your life.

*The first building block is your spiritual life.* We have learned how much God loves you. Jesus did everything necessary on the cross for you to be saved. He wants to have a deep and personal relationship with you. When you realize that Jesus is the only One who can meet the deep needs of your heart, then your relationships will balance out. If you are not continually developing your relationship with Jesus Christ by reading his Word, praying, and learning about him, you will not grow spiritually. Your spiritual condition is the foundation for your life. Everything else depends on that foundation. If you are not spiritually well, then the rest of your life will be in chaos. The decisions you make will not be wise, and you will end up with regret.

*The second building block is physical.* We learned through this study that God made you. He knew exactly how he wanted you to look. He thinks you are beautiful. He wants you to take care of the body he gave you. Your body is the temple of the Holy Spirit. He wants you to glorify him with your body. If you make choices that cause you to be physically unhealthy, this will affect other areas of your life. Many times when a teenage girl comes to me with depression and relationship problems, the first thing I ask her to do is visit her doctor for a physical checkup. Physical problems can cause depression and unclear thinking. Hormonal changes can cause emotions to be on a roller coaster. Being physically healthy is an important building block to achieve God's purpose in your life.

*The third building block is emotional.* Being healthy emotionally includes your self-esteem, how you feel in your heart about yourself, and how you feel about others, especially God. Protecting your heart and emotions is vitally important in being emotionally healthy. A broken heart affects your emotions and will in turn affect your relationships, your schoolwork, and your day-to-day routine. Placing your security in Christ will allow you the freedom to be yourself and not worry about what others think. Your emotional well-being affects everything you do.

*The fourth building block is mental.* This deals with how you think and process life in your mind. We talked about how addictions start in your mind. You think about the substance, person, or thing. You convince yourself that you need the thing or person you are thinking about. Then you act on what you have been thinking. How you think determines how you act. What you believe in your mind will set your standards, and your standards determine what decisions you make. Your decisions will determine if you will look back on life with regrets or not.

*The fifth and last building block is relational.* When all the other building blocks are properly in place, you will be able to relate well with other people. One of the most important things we talked about was how to love others. Love is an action, not a feeling. We need to get rid of childish ways as we grow so our love relationships will not be hindered.

Relationships are essential in your life. Every girl wants to be loved and respected by others. Every girl dreams of having that special person in her life who will love and cherish her. When all the building blocks are in the right place, love relationships will happen naturally.

How you get along with others will determine how effective you are in God's kingdom. God's plan for each of you is to help others, love others, and witness to others. When you are able to relate well and get along with and love others, you will look back on life with fewer regrets.

All of these building blocks are necessary to accomplish God's purpose in your life.

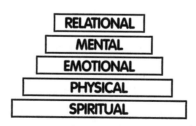

When you come to the end of your life, what do you want your husband, children, and friends to say about you? Do you want them to say you dressed sexy and acted sensual? Or do you want them to say you had nice hair and nails? Maybe you would like them to say you had more shoes in your closet than any woman they knew. I don't think so! Exactly what would you like them to say?

_____

_____

_____

_____

_____

_____

My friend Carol died six months after she was diagnosed with cancer. She was a wonderful Christian wife, mother, and teacher. She was a big influence in my life and in the lives of others who knew her as well.

At her funeral, the pastor told a story that happened earlier the same morning. It went something like this:

The phone rang in Carol's home. Her husband answered it, and an African-American lady said, "Mr. St. Clair, you don't know me. I work at the local grocery store where your wife shopped. I just wanted to let you know I am so saddened to learn of your wife's death. She was an incredible woman. When she came into the store, I always hoped she would come through my checkout lane. She always brightened my day, and I knew I had been loved when she left. In fact, all the cashiers at the store got together this morning and looked at her obituary together. We are all deeply sad."

Wow! That story touched my life. It made me want to live my life differently as a result. This story spoke volumes about Carol's life. Her family felt the same way. They didn't talk about frivolous things. They talked about what a godly mother and wife she was and other things that really count. I think Carol St. Clair lived her life with few regrets.

What about you? Will you make that commitment today? Maybe you are already living with some deep regret about decisions you have made in the past. Ask God's forgiveness. Forgive yourself. Then begin to do the things you have learned through this study. Will you begin from this day forward to make choices that will glorify God and honor your future husband, your future children, and your family for generations to come?

I have had a wonderful time with you the past few weeks. You have hung in there, and God has done wonderful things in your life. I wish I could give each of you a great big hug to let you know how proud I am of you.

I have a special prayer for you straight from God's Word.

When you come to the end of your life, may these words be said:

*Her children rise up and call her blessed; her husband also, and he praises her; "Many daughters have done well, but you exceed them all." Charm is deceitful and beauty is passing, but a woman who fears the Lord, she shall be praised. Give her of the fruit of her hands, and let her own works praise her in the gates.*

PROVERBS 31:28-31, NKJV

Better than that, when you stand before your Heavenly Father, he will look at you and say: "Well done, good and faithful servant.... Enter into the joy of your Lord" (Mt 25:23, NKJV).

**I will keep you in my heart until we meet again!**

# VIRTUAL YOU!

## Group Commitment

**I commit** to attend all mentoring/discipleship meetings faithfully.

**I commit** to complete all discipleship assignments faithfully.

**I commit** to keep confidential all personal information shared in mentoring/discipleship group.
*(I understand that any information shared regarding present abuse, suicide intent, or intent to harm another person is the legal responsibility of the adult in charge to report to the appropriate person.)*

**I commit** to keep myself pure in thought, word, and deed.

**I commit** to pray for other members of this group faithfully.

**I commit** to develop my relationship with Jesus Christ by having a regular quiet time, praying, and attending church.

Mentor _____    Mentor _____

Mentee _____    Mentee _____

Mentee _____    Mentee _____

Mentee _____    Mentee _____

Mentee _____    Mentee _____

Mentee _____    Mentee _____

Date_____

# Virtual You! Leader's Guide

If you are reading this Leader's Guide, you are probably already mentoring teenage girls or you are thinking about becoming a mentor. First, let me say, "Congratulations!" Mentoring preteen and teenage girls is one of the most important areas of service in which a Christian woman can be involved. May the Lord bless you as you pour your life into the lives of teenage girls.

Who are these girls and where do you find them? Many girls walk in and out of your life daily, many times unnoticed. When you open your eyes and look through God's glasses, you will see opportunities everywhere: your daughter and a few of her friends, teens in your church, girls in your neighborhood, or community organizations looking for volunteers.

Women's ministry is at an all-time high in American churches. Women are in crisis, and the church is ministering to them. That is wonderful. But would it not be more wonderful if women all across the world began to answer God's call from Titus, Chapter Two, and began to teach and train younger women to make wise decisions as they grow and mature?

We seldom think of preteen and teenage girls as women, but they are women-in-training. Girls are maturing much earlier today than even ten years ago. They are exposed to evil and are making poor choices at a younger age. We must reach and teach them earlier.

When mature women become serious about pouring our lives into preteen and teenage girls, we will raise up a new generation of women. Prevention ministry will eventually replace crisis intervention ministry.

## Guidelines for Leading a Small Group

As you begin to lead a small group of teenage girls through this twelve-week study of *Virtual You!* let me encourage you to pray for God's guidance in every word you say and every move you make. In today's world, the very lives of teenage girls are at risk. We need God's wisdom in reaching this generation of teens.

### Before You Begin

1. *Choose another woman to help you lead the group.* The best scenario for mentoring or discipling teenage girls is in small groups of four to eight girls with two adult women as leaders. You may want to choose a college girl or younger woman to help you. Teenage girls have three relationship needs: a relationship with God, a relationship with a significant adult, and healthy peer relationships. Mentoring groups meet these three needs.

2. *Meet initially with the girls to choose a place and time to meet weekly.* Send a note informing parents of the specifics, including the cost of the book to be used. (See the "Note to Parents" at the end of this book.) Choose a meeting time that is convenient for the girls and their parents, especially if the girls are not old enough to drive.

The place for your weekly meeting can be in your home, in the home of one of the girls, in a restaurant, at your church, or any place that will provide a good, comfortable atmosphere. If you meet in a restaurant, choose one where there will be few distractions. If you meet in one of the girls' homes, make sure the parents understand the girls need privacy to be able to talk freely.

Let me caution you against one area of concern. Please do not meet alone with one girl in your home, her home, or any other secluded place. If you need to meet one-on-one, make sure it is a semi-private place like a fast-food restaurant or your church where other people are in the same area. Protecting yourself against any accusation is vitally important. Many girls are carrying pain and baggage from the past. They may have deep hatred for their fathers or other men who have hurt them. Their thinking is confused by everything that has happened to them. Sometimes, they cannot differentiate between truth and fantasy. Spending time with a young girl in a private place will leave you defenseless if she accuses you of something immoral or unethical. You may think the situation is harmless and suddenly find you are facing a false accusation. It is always better to be safe than sorry.

3. *Start your meetings on time and end on time.* You will need about an hour and thirty minutes to adequately cover the material. If a girl needs to stay after the meeting and talk, make sure she has permission from her parents.

4. *Lead the girls in setting up guidelines for the meeting.*
   Some suggestions are:
   - *Respect the person who is talking. Don't talk while others are talking.* (In one group I led in the past, the rule was, "The person holding Jimmie's set of keys may talk." The girls loved throwing the keys back and forth.)
   - *No visitors or additional girls until a new study begins.* Girls need the freedom to talk openly and feel they have confidentiality. If new people come in or visitors show up, it may hinder that freedom. If a new person is added after the study begins, make sure she also signs the Commitment page in the book.

**During the Meetings**

1. *Always begin and end your meeting with prayer.* Modeling prayer and teaching girls how to pray is an important part of mentoring.

Ask the girls to write their prayer requests on sticky notes for you each week. This will help you know how to pray for your girls each day, what their needs are, what is going on in their lives, and how to better relate to them individually.

If you take prayer requests openly, make sure it is a personal request. Do not allow girls to use this as a gossip session. You are in control of what goes on in the meetings. Do not allow names of those not present to be mentioned. Do not talk about situations that can hurt the reputation of another person.

2. *Hold the girls accountable for their quiet times, doing their lessons, memorizing their verses, and their behavior during the week.* The following questions may be used as accountability questions:

- Did you have your quiet time this week?
- Tell me about your emotions this week. Did you follow your heart? Or did you follow God?
- How did you exercise and how were your eating habits?
- Have you done anything you need to confess to God this week?
- Are you lying about any of the above?
- How did you develop your godly character this week?

3. *Guide girls in staying to the point.* Of course, you will always want to be sensitive to the Holy Spirit. There may be a time when you have to drop the lesson and address a specific need, but those times will be few.

4. *Allow time for talking and fun.* The girls need to know that when they come in there will be snacks on the counter, and they can talk and play around for fifteen minutes. At that time, the meeting will begin and it's time to focus. This will allow them to release their energy. If they are late, they will miss the snacks only. On the other hand, if you serve the snacks first, some girls may be more prone to leave early. You have to know your girls and what works for them.

5. *During the meeting stick to a reasonable schedule.* Don't spend all your time taking prayer requests, or spend all your time on one question.

## What to Do Each Week

### Week One: Preliminary Meeting
Decide where you will meet and when you will meet, get to know each other, set up the guidelines, etc. You might want to meet at a fun restaurant.

### Week Two: Introduction
- Set up snacks on the counter and allow girls to fellowship.
- Make sure each girl feels welcome and is not left standing alone. (15 minutes)
- Begin the session in prayer asking God to bless each girl present, to guide you as a leader, to help the girls grow close to God and to each other. (5 minutes)
- Welcome the girls to the Mentoring Group. Ask each girl to introduce herself and explain why she decided to join this mentoring group. (10 minutes)

- Give out the books and collect money unless the girls have paid previously. (5 minutes)
- Explain the Group Commitment and give each girl an opportunity to sign on page 157 in the book. (15 minutes)
- Give a brief overview of the book. (15 minutes)
- Ask the girls to read Chapter One, "Which Sticky Note Did I Write My Password On?" for next week. Explain that the ❤ symbol indicates the theme verse they are to memorize during the week. You may want to offer a small gift or reward system if they learn the verses. The ❤ reminds them the verses are from God's love letter to each of them individually. Explain that the ☺ symbols indicate the questions to be discussed each week in the session. Assure each girl she will not be forced to answer any question. It will be on a volunteer basis only. During the sessions make sure each girl has an opportunity to talk if she chooses. Don't let any one girl monopolize the discussion. (10 minutes)
- Close the session in prayer, asking the girls to share any prayer requests they may have. (10 minutes)

**Weeks Three Through Twelve**

The following schedule may be followed for weeks three through twelve:

**1. Fellowship time** (15 minutes)

This time can be used for fellowship, light refreshments, and late-comer arrival.

**2. Prayer time** (15 minutes)

Allow girls to share prayer requests. This can be done in several ways.

- If you take prayer requests openly in the group, remind the girls to limit this to personal requests and to be brief and to the point. (This will prevent the urge to gossip about the problems of others not present and will keep the group on schedule.) As the girls talk, write their prayer requests in your prayer journal, so you can pray for them during the week.

- When the girls arrive, pass out index cards on which to write their prayer requests. You may choose to keep the cards to have an idea how to pray for the girls during the week. Occasionally ask them to exchange cards and pray for each other during the week.

- Give each girl a prayer journal. Openly take prayer requests and give girls time to write each other's requests down so they can pray for each other during the week. (This method takes the most time during the group meeting, but is a wonderful way to teach the girls how to intercede for each other.)

**3. Discussion** (40 minutes)

(See Week-by-Week Discussion Guide)


**4. Accountability time** (15 minutes)

Divide the girls into two smaller groups with an adult leading the Accountability Time.

- Allow girls to recite their memory verses♥ for that week.
- Ask each girl the following accountability questions.
    - a) Did you have your quiet time faithfully this week?
    - b) Did you guard your heart and emotions this week?
    - c) Did you develop your godly character this week?
    - e) Did you lie about any of the above?
- Encourage girls to meet with you at another time if they need to talk about personal issues.

**5. Closing prayer** (5 minutes)

Bring the girls back together to close in prayer. Ask one person to close in prayer or ask each girl to say a sentence prayer if time allows.

The Week-by-Week Discussion Guide that follows will help you lead the discussions each week. Pray during the week that God will work in your life in a way that you will have personal examples or stories to begin each discussion time. Be careful not to "air your dirty laundry" or use the group as a "counseling group" for yourself. If you have personal problems, make sure those are addressed and dealt with at another time.

## Week-by-Week Discussion Guide

### Week Three
*Chapter One: "Which Sticky Note Did I Write My Password On?"*

- Try to find a larger-than-normal key as a visual. Hold the key up and ask, "What is the purpose of this key?" (Answers will vary from locking up something to letting someone free.) Accept all answers. Give every girl an opportunity to answer. When one girl answers, your response should be, "Okay, what does someone else think?" or "That sounds good, what are some other possibilities?" This will encourage the girls to think. If you say, "Right!" the other girls will shut down and stop thinking. Make this a practice in every session.
- Lead the girls to think about the security and freedom keys give. This will lead into the discussion about the importance of protecting their hearts during their teen years.

- Continue the discussion, focusing on the ☺ questions. Be sure you touch on the topics of salvation, not putting their security in a guy, and forgiving those who have hurt them. You may choose to discuss questions not marked with a smiley face. Be careful not to discuss questions generating private topics not appropriate for group discussion.

- Wrap up the session with this statement: "If you have never put your trust in Jesus Christ as your Savior, you will continue to feel that emptiness in your heart. You can try to fill it with guys, sex, dating, sports, drugs, alcohol, looks, or anything else, but you will never be satisfied until you ask Christ into your life and have a personal relationship with him. If you have never done that, I will be happy to talk with you after we finish the session tonight."

- Remind the girls to read Chapter Two, "Click Onto a Real Relationship," for next week.

**Week Four**

*Chapter Two: "Click Onto a Real Relationship"*

- Start the discussion time by giving your testimony. Be sure you use words the girls will understand. Don't use hard theological terms. Be simple.

- Move on to the ☺ questions in Chapter Two. Give each girl the opportunity to give her testimony.

- If a girl is reluctant to give her testimony, you may want to go through the ABC's of salvation at the end of the session. Please do not single girls out or embarrass them in any way. Ask the girls to bow their heads and close their eyes. Ask if every girl is sure she has asked Jesus into her heart. If not, ask if she would like to receive Jesus at this time. If so, pray with those who would like to accept Christ. Many times in asking teens to share their testimony, they will realize they do not have one because they have never accepted Christ.

- Remind the girls to read Chapter Three, "Who's in Your Chat Room?" for next week.

## Week Five
*Chapter Three: "Who's in Your Chat Room?"*
- Discuss the ☺ questions.
- At the appropriate time ask one of the girls to read "Every Good Book Has a Love Story" using expression. Ask the girls to tell something from the story they had never thought about before.
- Continue discussing the ☺ questions.
- Go over the Quiet Time Guide. Answer any questions the girls have. Encourage them to spend time alone with God every day this week.
- Remind the girls to read Part One of Chapter Four, "Has Your Purity Code Been Hacked?" for next week.

## Week Six
*Chapter Four: "Has Your Purity Code Been Hacked?" Part One*
This chapter is the longest chapter in the book and tends to promote a lot of discussion. You may want to divide this chapter into two sessions. A good dividing place begins with "God's Security Zone."
- Discuss abstinence versus purity.
- Go to the ☺ questions on why to have sex or why not to have sex. Write the girls' answers on butcher or flip chart paper. You will use this at the end of the session. Explain you are

asking these questions to help them learn how to make wise decisions in their lives.

- Briefly talk about the section titled "Light My Fire." Some girls have the misconception that sex is dirty. It's important to explain the difference in sex used for God's purpose and sex used for the wrong reasons.

- Discuss the three areas affected by sex before marriage (body, mind, and soul). Use Shannon's story to bring these three areas to life. Ask questions such as "How did sex before marriage with Zack affect Shannon's body?" "How did sex before marriage affect Shannon's mind?" "How did sex before marriage affect Shannon's soul?" "How did sex with Shannon affect Zack's soul?"

- Refer back to the "Reasons to Have Sex" and "Reasons Not to Have Sex" written on butcher paper. Ask the girls their thoughts now regarding their answers. Do they feel differently? How will this affect decisions they will make regarding sexual purity in the future?

- Close the session in prayer. Remind each girl to read Part Two of Chapter Four for next week.

**Week Seven**

*Chapter Four: "Has Your Purity Code Been Hacked?" Part Two*

- Many times we tell girls to strive for purity or not to have sex, but we don't tell them how to be pure. There are several steps they can take to protect their purity. During this session, you will work through these steps.

- Ask the ☺ question, "Why do you think God's rules are so specific about sex outside of marriage? Do you think he wants to spoil your fun?"

171

- Discuss the "breastplate of righteousness." Make sure the girls understand God's precept that righteousness protects their hearts from the consequences of personal sin.
- Introduce the "Virtual Kiss-Off" by asking the ☺ question, "What does a kiss mean?" Be sure not to make the legalistic rule, "no kissing." This is a huge turn-off to girls and causes a rebellious attitude. They need to make this decision and decide if they will save their kisses or not. Helping girls set up the goal to strive for purity works more efficiently than telling girls what they "shouldn't do."
- Ask the ☺ question, "When a guy whispers 'I love you,' what does it mean to you?" Discuss how saving the words "I love you" can protect a girl's heart and her purity.
- Introduce the section on temptation by asking one of the girls to retell the story about the lion. Discuss ways to avoid temptation. Discuss how avoiding temptation can foster a life of purity.
- Assure the girls of God's forgiveness when they confess their sins and turn from it.
- Briefly touch on sexual abuse, making sure the girls understand that past sexual abuse is not their fault. If abuse is going on at the present, encourage them to tell an adult. Many times this will spark the courage for a girl to get help. It is not wise to talk in length about examples of sexual abuse or your own personal experiences in this area. You never want to put ideas in the mind of a teen. If one of the girls tells you she is being sexually abused at this time, it is vitally important for you to report the abuse. If you are mentoring through a church program, go to the pastor or youth pastor for advice. Many churches have a reporting plan. Know the laws in your

state regarding your responsibility to report. Many times a teen will say, "I have something to tell you, but you can't tell anyone." You should never make a promise of confidentiality you cannot keep. Your reply can be something like this, "The things you tell me I will keep confidential unless I believe you are in danger of hurting yourself or someone else, or a minor is being sexually abused. Then I will only tell the person or persons who need to know." The most important thing is protection of the girl. Don't confront the abuser. By doing so you may be putting the life of the girl in danger.

- Close the session by presenting the three categories at the end of this session. Allow girls to volunteer the category into which they fit and what decisions they have made. Pray for each girl individually after she shares her commitment.

- Remind the girls to read Chapter Five, "Cracking the Code on Guys," for next week.

### Week Eight
*Chapter Five: "Cracking the Code on Guys"*

- ☺ Name characteristics of the guy you want to marry.

- ☺ Name characteristics of the kind of girl a godly guy wants to marry. Do you spend time trying to catch your guy or developing godly character? Which do you think will work the best?

- Have one of the girls read Ashley's story. You may know of similar stories to share.

- ☺ Ask the girls to talk about "red flags" Ashley should have noticed. "Why do you think it was hard for Ashley to see Kirk's faults? How can you protect yourself from being in the same situation?" (Bring up the character questions to ask before dating or marrying a guy.)

173

- ☺ Have each girl share the dating standards she chose. This might be a good time to give each girl a pretty piece of paper on which to write her standards and decorate for her room. (This makes a good "sleepover" activity also.)
- Remind the girls to read Chapter Six, "The Reality of Virtue," for next week.

## Week Nine

*Chapter Six: "The Reality of Virtue"*

- Start the discussion with the caterpillar/butterfly example. Explain that God wants to do a miracle makeover not only on how each girl looks and dresses but inside as well.
- Discuss the ☺ questions. Let each girl describe one thing she would like to change about herself.
- Discuss ☺ questions on sex and the media.
- Ask girls to describe what they have seen in fashion magazines that has influenced them toward looking and acting sexy.
- Ask girls to read the first three ☺ Proverbs references and tell how this woman with no character got the attention of men.
- Discuss 1 Corinthians 6:18 and ask each girl to tell how this verse has changed her perspective.
- Ask the girls to briefly look over Proverbs 31 and tell how they think guys would be different if their mothers taught them how to choose a wife based on these verses. Emphasize these are the things King Lemuel's mother taught him. King Lemuel is thought by some Bible scholars to be the same person as King Solomon. If so, we know that King Solomon was very wise. How should this affect how they choose a boyfriend and husband?
- ☺ What does it mean that beauty is fleeting and charm is deceptive?

- Say, "However a girl gets a guy, she will have to continue the same to keep him." Ask, "What do you think that means?"
- Ask the girls to name characteristics that should be avoided, found in Galatians 5:19-21.
- Ask the girls to name characteristics that come from the Holy Spirit, found in Galatians 5:22-23.
- End the session by talking about the inevitable struggles we will all face in life. Talk about the story of the butterfly struggling to get out of the cocoon. When going through struggles, depending on God's strength and developing godly character will mold us into persons of beauty from the inside out.
- Remind the girls to read Chapter Seven, "Search Engine for True Love," for next week.

### Week Ten
*Chapter Seven: "Search Engine for True Love"*
- Ask each girl to give her definition for love ☺ at the beginning of the chapter.
- Briefly go through the steps of learning how to love. Explain that the steps are very important and should not be skipped.
- Ask the girls to look at the ☺ on 1 Corinthians and tell what they wrote about God's definition of love. How does that differ from their definition?
- Discuss at length putting away childish things. Ask the girls to name childish ways. Ask them to name childish ways in their lives. Explain the importance of putting away childish things to prevent destroying their love relationships. Go through this section and explain in detail so the girls will understand. This is a vital part of learning to love.

- Discuss the difference between true love and infatuation. Use Tiffany's story to bring out important points.
- Ask, "When will you know if the guy you are dating is the one God has for you?" (Time, commitment, actions, character, God reveals it to you, your parents' blessing, etc.)
- Remind the girls to read Chapter Eight, "Access Your Positives" for next week.

## Week Eleven

*Chapter Eight: "Access Your Positives"*

- Ask the girls to define absolute truth.
- Ask the girls to define principles.
- Ask the girls to name the three absolute truths discussed in this chapter. "How does God feel about you, and what part did he have in your birth? How will these three absolute truths change the way you see yourself?"
- ☺ What does the Bible mean when it says, "You are bought with a price?" Ask, "To whom do your body and spirit belong?"
- ☺ Name ways you can glorify God in the areas named.
- Ask the girls to name ways they should have control over their bodies.
- Discuss Principles 1-8. Explain to the girls how these basic principles can help them make wise choices in how they dress and look.
- Many adults are asking for ways to influence the way girls are dressing. Use the questions regarding guys dressing in muscle shirts and tight swim trunks to help girls get the picture.
- Some people say God looks at the heart and not at the appearance. How do you think your heart condition will affect your appearance?

- Remind the girls to read the Conclusion, "From Girls to Women With Few Regrets," for next week.

**Week Twelve**
*Conclusion: "From Girls to Women With Few Regrets"*
   Follow the basic schedule but use the discussion time as a working review session. Provide pretty sheets of 8 1/2 x 11-inch paper and slim colored markers. Ask the girls to write their epitaph in detail. Encourage them to decorate it and put it up in their room where they can see if often. Discuss the importance of making decisions each day that will enable them to look back on life with few regrets.
   Close the session by allowing each girl to share what she has learned during the study. Allow each girl to pray, thanking God for what she has learned.

**After You Complete the Study:**
Decide if you will continue the group and begin a new study or if this is the last session.

### Additional Suggestions for Leaders

- Keep a daily prayer journal for each girl. Give her your written prayers for her life at the end of the last session.
- E-mails and instant messages are great, but a handwritten note occasionally is special. One youth minister wrote a note to one of the youth in his church before a significant track meet. She won and had a plaque made with pictures, her medal, and his note placed on it. It was something tangible she could hold in her hand.

- Occasionally, meet in a different place that has significant meaning. For example, when talking about God's love, meet beside a public fountain. Compare God's love to the fountain that continually flows. Each time those girls pass the fountain they will be reminded of God's love.

- Give each girl a "quiet time basket" with all the things she will need to do her quiet time each day. Suggested items: A pen, journal, devotional book, Bible (unless girls already have a special Bible they use), tissues, CD with worship music. It really depends on your budget. You may give them items to add to their basket occasionally. This would make a perfect Christmas gift, if you are meeting around the holidays.

## Note to Parents

Dear Parents,

We look forward to the time we will spend with your daughter during the next twelve weeks in our mentoring/discipleship group. *Virtual You!* is a fun, interactive study that will draw your daughter into a closer relationship with Jesus Christ.

Teenage girls have three relationship needs: a relationship with God, relationships with significant adults, and healthy peer relationships. Mentoring groups foster all of these relationship needs.

We will use *Virtual You!* and the Bible as our curriculum. The girls will read one chapter per week and answer thought-provoking questions related to the material. Each chapter includes a memory verse. We will meet once a week to discuss the material, for accountability, and for fellowship.

Your daughter will get as much out of the group as she puts into it. Commitment to regular attendance, memory work, reading the book, and answering questions will make this study more meaningful and helpful in your daughter's life.

Thank you for allowing us to be part of your daughter's life. We covet your support and prayers as we lead the group. Below you will find important information relating to the logistics of the group.

Again, thank you for entrusting your precious daughter into our care during this time. If we can ever help you or your daughter in any way, please feel free to call one of us.

Blessings to you and your family!

(Signatures) _____

_____

_____

Beginning date: _____Ending Date:_____
Meeting Place: _____
Adult Leader _____Phone_____
Adult Leader _____Phone_____

Please have your daughter bring $_____ to the next group meeting to cover the cost of the book. Thank you.

*(Permission to photocopy granted)*

# Notes

## Chapter Five
### *Cracking the Code on Guys*

1. From "Domestic Violence: The Facts—A Handbook to STOP the Violence," (Boston: Battered Women Fighting Back).
2. Ibid.
3. Report of the American Psychological Association Presidential Task Force on Violence and the Family, APA, 1996.
4. Dr. Allen Jackson, Professor of Youth Ministry, New Orleans Theological Seminary.

## Chapter Eight
### *Access Your Positives!*

1. Roberta Larson Duyff, *The American Dietetic Association's Complete Food and Nutrition Guide* (Minneapolis: Chronimed, 1996), 8.

For More Information

The author is available for speaking engagements.
For more information, call or write:

Jimmie L. Davis
P.O. Box 170568
Spartanburg, SC 29301

www.girlsministry.org
jimmie@teleplex.net
AOLIM: VirtualYou77